Piper and Shelly and the Weird Thing That Happened

Russell Holbrook

Published by Splatterpiece Press, 2024.

This is a work of fiction. Similarities to real people, places, or events are entirely coincidental.

PIPER AND SHELLY AND THE WEIRD THING THAT HAPPENED

First edition. January 2, 2024.

ISBN: 979-8224335725

Written by Russell Holbrook.

Table of Contents

Valkos's Special Dedication Department has approved this book's dedication to Mandy De Sandra, who has always encouraged me in my quest for Gnostic truth and enlightenment.

One. Tuesday Evening, Mable Town Food Truck Park

. . . .

"**H**oly Mohamed on a meat hook this is forking delicious!" Piper said, squeezing the words out of her full mouth. She snatched another piece of funnel cake off the flimsy paper plate and crammed it into her bulging cheeks.

"Fork yeah it is, for real," Shelly agreed. "Gypsies make the best funnel cakes".

"M'm-M-M! Giddydamn Gypsies, they're forking culinary wizards," Piper added.

She chewed. He chewed. They relished.

Piper looked at Shelly with glassy eyes that beamed affection and contentment. "I'm so glad we came to food truck Tuesday, Shelly," she said tenderly.

"Me too, Piper," Shelly agreed.

Piper was going in for yet another chunk of greasy goodness when she spotted something out of place on the dessert. Her fingers stopped and hovered, trembling over the fried delicacy. Her eyes glowed bright pink and blew up into giant bulbs four times their normal size. Insanely bright, hot pink lasers shot out of Piper's glowing orbs.

Shelly threw a hand over his face to shield himself from the blinding light. "Ow, Piper, turn down your eyes, you're blinding me!"

"Fork, Shelly! Quit whining and give me a second to find my sunglasses!"

Piper rummaged through her Valkos brand Ladies' Tote Box that sat next to her on the picnic table bench, the lasers from her eyes shooting out in all directions.

An unfortunate squirrel was hit by Piper's laser beams on his way to pick up an acorn. He was horrified as well as abruptly and unexpectedly blinded. The squirrel had no insurance to protect against sudden blindness by random laser attacks. He knew he was screwed. His heart sank. He thought of suicide but he remembered that his life insurance policy didn't cover that either.

He sighed. *I guess I'll just wander out in front of traffic, it's not like I could see a car coming anyway. It will be ruled an accidental death and my family can collect the insurance money and little Tardy, my dearest daughter, can afford her private school tuition.*

The sad squirrel turned and walked away, following the sounds of the nearby four-lane road to guide him to his death. *Goodbye sweet world*, he thought to himself. On the way to the road, he sang the squirrel's lament and all the nearby animals took note of his sorrow.

"Aha- Found the forkers!" Piper said. She pulled out her oversized prescription sunglasses and pushed them over her eyes.

Once the sunglasses were snug on Piper's face, the blistering pink light subsided. Shelly lowered his hands. "Geez, Piper, what's with the angry eyes?"

"There's a forking hair in my funnel cake! Fork! Giddydamn Gypsies, they're such careless culinary wizards!"

"*Our* funnel cake, Piper. But yeah, that is forking grody." Shelly leaned in to inspect the powdered sugar-covered delight. That's when he saw it: the protruding tip of a human hair in the center of the funnel cake.

Shelly squealed. Heebie-jeebies popped out of his pores and crawled over his skin. He screeched and batted at his arms. "Heebie-jeebies! Heebie-jeebies! Get 'em off me! Get 'em off! Help, Piper, help!"

"Sit still!" Piper commanded. "I'll get 'em!"

Shelly gripped the picnic bench and tried to keep from shivering as the small, pea-soup green, roach-like creatures crawled all over his body.

"Close your eyes, Shell, and say something that will make me get super-pissed. I can feel my eyes cooling down."

Shelly squeezed his eyes shut and shouted, "No equal rights for Ninjas! They're a lower class and they don't deserve to walk among us. Separate! Segregate!" He shut his mouth just before the bugs could crawl inside him.

Hot steam shot out of Piper's ears. She slammed her fists on the table. Her bulbous eyes smoldered. She raised her sunglasses. Rays of hot pink light showered Shelly, bathing him in an ultra-bright glow. He winced at the heat. He giggled as the bugs sizzled and dropped off his body. Then, Shelly heard Piper popping the lock on her Ladies' Carrying Tote. He waited, holding himself still.

"It's okay now Shelly, they're all gone," Piper said, her voice soft and sweet.

Shelly opened his eyes. Piper had taken her sunglasses off and wore a happy expression. Shelly exhaled and relaxed. "Thanks, Piper, for reals."

Piper smiled and nodded. "No problem, Shell."

She picked up the paper plate that sat between them and pulled at the hair in the middle of the cake. A long, jet-black strand snaked out from beneath the powdered sugar. Piper held it up and inspected it in the sodium lamps of the food truck park. "Now this, this is a forking problem."

Piper's face wrinkled. She shook her hand and the hair floated away on the cool evening breeze. With her face twisted in knots, Piper sat down the plate and shoved the cake to Shelly.

"Take it back! I want a new one! And tell those Gypsy forks to keep their greasy forking Gypsy hairs out of my funnel cake!" Piper fumed. A slight glimmer came back into her eyes, sending sparks of pink light dancing over her sallow cheeks. She scrubbed her hands against her faded orange corduroy pants, exhaled hard, and pushed her shoulder-length, frazzled, electric-blue hair back behind her ears.

"Don't worry, Piper, I'll take care of it," Shelly said.

With an audible sigh, tall, lanky Shelly, who had no concept of urgency, and who hated all forms of confrontation, reluctantly slid off the picnic table bench, the befouled cake in hand.

He slouched to the Gypsy pastry truck and stood waiting for someone to come to the window and bear his complaint. His pale, pronounced nose took in the aroma of the food truck: a dense swirl of deep-fried dough, sugar, and fat. His tall ears that jutted out from under his choppy mess of bright green hair listened to the voices echoing from an unseen part of the mammoth vehicle, which seemed more like a ramshackle house on wheels than a legitimate food truck. The voices spoke a strange poetry, chanting in a foreign tongue. The odd language raised the hairs on the back of his neck. *What are they doing back there? And shouldn't someone be working the window?*

Shelly glanced around the food truck park. Several other smiling couples occupied tables across the lot. A happy family of four sat in chairs under the park's fake palm tree. And there was Piper, alone at the table, gazing down at her phone, giggling. They all seemed so far away.

A cool wind blew against Shelly. Faint fear hissed at his spine. From deep within the truck, the pop and crackle of frying dough floated by. The chanting grew louder. The wind blew colder against his skin. The smiles of the couples and the family turned into a mess of blood and broken teeth. Their eyes became burned-out holes. Piper's giggles turned into desperate, raspy gagging. The grease popped and sang, louder and louder as if it was inside Shelly's head. Louder, louder! It burned his mind. He gasped.

A small, elderly Gypsy woman with a shock of long, pure white hair appeared at the window holding a fresh, powdered sugar-dusted funnel cake in her hands. Shelly jumped.

"Here you are my dear," the ancient woman said. She held the flimsy paper plate out to Shelly.

"But I haven't ordered yet," Shelly said, confused. He sat the soiled funnel cake just inside the window. "There was a hair in it, a long, black hair."

"My niece, she is so careless. We tell her to wear the hat but she says no," the old woman said. Her spotted, wrinkled hands shook and threatened to spill the pastry onto the ground. "You take this one," the wizened woman said, grinning and nodding at the fresh dessert. "You'll like it much, much better. Yes, a taste you will never, ever forget!" The ancient gypsy smiled wide, revealing her severe lack of teeth, and laughed hysterically, her eyes bulging in their sunken sockets.

Unnerved by the gypsy woman's outburst, the skin on Shelly's back began to crawl. Knowing that his skin was trying to get away from him again and seeing what a problem that could be on date night, Shelly slapped his back hard with his free hand until his skin yelped and became still. Slowly, he reached out and took the fresh funnel cake from the gypsy woman's shaky hands.

The gypsy lady turned away. Her shrill laughter echoed as she disappeared to the back of the truck.

Shelly called into the food truck window. "Hey, how did you..." his voice dropped off to a whisper. "How did you know I wanted a new cake?"

Shelly craned his neck up to the food truck window and listened again. He heard bubbling grease, several whispering voices, and gleeful cackling. The sounds of low, jubilant laughter filled Shelly with unease. His stomach turned.

Giddydamn Gypsies, Shelly thought. *They're so weird but they make the best forking funnel cakes!*

Shelly sloughed off his apprehension and took the replacement funnel cake back to the table where Piper was browsing OutSpace on her Smarty-Pants Millennial Edition Smarty Phone Version 17.0. She looked up when Shelly reached the table.

"Oh, yums that was fast!" She said, her eyes feasting on the piping hot new funnel cake. "Thanks, baby."

"No worries." Shelly looked down at Piper's phone. "Are you checking the Chaz Luger stats again?"

"Fork yeah, I am! You won't believe it; he's up to 218 for this segment."

"Flex! That guy's unstoppable!" Shelly cried out in astonishment.

"Mad respect, I know!" Piper grabbed at the funnel cake. "Let's eat this forker!"

Shelly held off. With the sound of the gypsies' cackling still playing in his mind, he let Piper take the first bite. She tore off a piece of the funnel cake, eased it into her mouth, chewed and moaned, and proclaimed, "Mmmmmm... Fork me flying on a broomstick this is some for real scrummy scrum!"

Needing no further convincing that the new cake was as safe as it was surely delicious, Shelly snagged a chunk and shoved it in his salivating pie-hole. An explosion of sugary, fatty, greasy wonder filled his mouth. His taste buds went into orgasmic overload. Drool seeped from the corners of his mouth. His eyes rolled. His penis twitched. He testified. "Wow, it's unbelievable -this is even better than the first one!"

Euphoria melted Shelly's senses and wiped all his cares away. His feet went numb and he floated on happy clouds of pastry-induced bliss. He mumbled and groaned and swayed in his seat, not feeling the bench beneath him. Neither Shelly nor Piper could speak. All they could do or wanted to do was eat. And so, they did, scarfing down the glorious pastry until it was gone.

"That was amazingly delicious," Shelly mumbled, wiping his lips with his hand and then licking his hand.

"Yeah, it totally was," Piper slurred. She stared at Shelly, smiling and content, wave after crashing wave of comforting warmth spreading over her body. She smacked her lips in slow motion. Her eyes glazed over and she squeaked out a small yawn. She folded her hands in her lap, sighed, and slumped forward, smiling from ear to ear.

Shelly was staring up into the darkening orange and purple evening sky. Piper was giggling. There was the sound of clothing being wrestled away from skin. Shelly's eyelids flapped heavily like gigantic wet wings. He lowered his gaze to Piper. She was completely naked, straddling the picnic table bench.

He was standing before her: Mable Town's most beloved adult film star, Chaz Luger. His massive hunk of man meat slid in and out between Piper's thin, sloppy, wet lips.

Piper's eyes rolled back in her head. She moaned and stroked the huge rod as it glided back and forth. Testicles as big as regulation-size tennis balls, with professionally braided cords of pubic hair, rested safely in her free hand.

Shelly's respectably sized member hardened as he looked on in a trance, in total awe of the sight before him.

"Chaz Luger..." Shelly mumbled in disbelief.

The legendary adult film star flashed his trademark brilliant white smile and winked at Shelly. "Hey there buddy! This girlyirly of yours is a real cum huffer! She sucks it like a total pro!"

Pride washed over Shelly. *That's my girlyirly, mine, tackling the tube steak of a legend,* he mused.

Chaz Luger ran his fingers through Piper's greasy electric blue locks. His perfectly toned ass checks flexed and relaxed and flexed and relaxed as he moved in rhythm with Piper's strokes of her lips and hands and the licks of her tongue. Chaz let his hands travel down to Piper's nipples and knead them gently between his fingers before stroking and massaging the underside of her perfectly proportioned breasts.

"You know, I do love the young ones," Chaz said to Shelly. His words crawled out in slow motion. His eyes sagged heavily with chemically enhanced lust.

Shelly smiled at an unexpected touch. Soft, warm hands lighted on his shoulders. A voice

carried on hot breath whispered in his ear. "Shelly, take me with your manly man wood! Make my dreams come true!"

Shelly swiveled. His eyes burst wide in wonder. His dick started screaming.

"Holy forking forkers!" Shelly's penis screamed from inside his pants.

Sometimes Shelly wished that he hadn't been born with a talking penis, but most of the time it was pretty cool, especially in party situations. His face mouth hung open in silent shock and wonder. He said, "It is Mistress Ivanna Swallow- Mable Town's most beloved and respected Goddess of the Night!"

Sweat broke on Shelly's brow. His hands shook with reverent fear.

Mistress Ivanna Swallow stood naked before him. From her waist-length auburn hair to her mountainous round breasts to her toned stomach to her curvaceous hips, down the reach of her long legs to her professionally manicured toenails, every inch of her flesh covered in sparkling golden spray-on tan, her perfect body radiated angelic splendor.

"Oh, holy mistress, our sacred Goddess of the Night, please give me the honor of serving you," Shelly said with his face mouth. He swung off the picnic table bench and fell to his knees.

The mistress smiled down at him. "Do not be afraid, young one. I've had this moment marked in my date book since you were a child. I worked everything out with your parents. They've been making monthly payments of $19.95 ever since you were in second grade. Now is the time for you to become one with The Night."

"Monthly installments of $19.95? Damn, that's sexy!" Shelly said. "I always knew my parents cared about my future!"

Shelly thrust his face between Ivanna's thighs, deep into her untamed bush. He inhaled deeply. The musky intoxication floated through him.

Ivanna scooted up on the table and leaned back with her legs spread high and wide. She called out to the Lord Allah, who, at that time happened to be sitting in the clouds taking a poo.

When the Lord Allah heard Ivanna's voice, he parted the clouds and looked down at her. He swelled with pride. *There's my girlyirly*! He smiled and winked and blew her a kiss.

In that moment Ivanna's full power manifested itself and she squirted onto Shelly's face. Shelly moaned as the hot wet viscous spread over his skin, mouth, and eyes and kept spreading and growing until the ooey gooey love sauce covered his entire head. All the hairs on Shelly's body stood on end. He felt chills. The sticky hot lady lava oozed over Shelly, eating away at his clothes and caressing his body like a thousand invisible hands. Suddenly, he sensed his cock waving in the wind.

"Woo-hoo, I'm free baby, I'm free!" Shelly's penis exclaimed.

He felt the evening air on his naked body. Over the towering mounds of Ivanna Swallow's immaculate breasts, he saw Piper bent over the table. Chaz Luger was behind her, plowing her nubile flesh. Shelly felt such admiration for Piper at that moment that it was hard to concentrate on Ivanna's beautiful spaces. He had to look away. The sounds of Piper's moans played lovely melodies in his ears.

Ivanna's lady jizz pooled over Shelly's anus, solidified, and molded itself into a ten-inch disembodied liquid lady dick. Controlling the phantom member with her mind, Ivanna worked it into Shelly. He winced as the liquid cock pushed inside him.

Shelly moved his mouth over Ivanna's engorged clit and drew it up between his lips while the watery ghost dick rammed his theretofore unexplored ass. Shelly squirmed and moaned. He felt the hammering phantasmagoric purple-headed love rod slip deep inside him. It floated through his body, past his spirit, and merged into his aching meat stick.

And as it was in the beginning of the Earth, the two cocks became one flesh.

Shelly blinked. He was up, standing on the picnic table bench. Ivanna was on her back next to him, sprawled sideways across the table, reciting her favorite stanzas from "Le Petite Le Faun". Chaz Luger had Shelly's man meat in his mouth, slurping and sucking and threatening to inhale Shelly whole.

Chaz moved away from Shelly and spread out on the table. Piper crawled on top of him. He rested his head on the Mistress' chest while Piper eased herself down onto the full length of his legendary shaft, pulling the entirety of his majesty inside her. Piper moaned and lifted her hands in praise. Shelly joined in and became a part of the writhing flesh puzzle. He hoisted Ivanna's legs in the air and thrust deep into her. His cock crooned with joy as it slid in and out of the Mistress in a delicate rhythm. His eyes shot back and forth from Piper to Chaz to Ivanna and back again. Shelly almost couldn't believe what was happening; it was the most beautiful moment of his life.

A twenty-four-piece marching band comprised of kazoos, car horns, disembodied screams, crashing cymbals, banging drums, and recorders played in the distance, hammering out an inverted polka. The grand noise caught Shelly's attention. His ears twitched and twisted and searched for the source of the sound. It seemed to be coming from deep inside the Gypsy food truck, as if from an out-of-tune transistor radio. He glanced at the truck. Ancient, withered Gypsy women began filing out the back door, each one carrying a golden plate that was piled high with steaming hot, glistening funnel cakes.

Hunger burned inside Shelly. Piper smelled the holy aroma, too. She held out her arms like a starving baby and begged the Gypsy women to bring the precious cakes to her. The old women smiled and sang as they came near. With loving hands, they fed Piper while she rode on top of her all-time favorite adult actor.

The Gypsies surrounded Shelly and Ivanna. One by one they tore a piece of cake off and fed it to the viral young man. And more Gypsies came out with more cakes. And Shelly and Piper ate and ate and ate until the golden plates were empty. There was a great thunder crack and the sky turned red. Shelly thrust faster and faster and Piper rode Chaz as hard and fast as she could, her rhythm setting new world records and standards of excellence with every passing moment.

Piper and Shelly locked eyes.

"Oh, Shell!" Piper shouted.

"Oh fork, Piper!" Shelly screamed.

They roared and exploded and reached for the unattainable and together they went blind, sucked into the breath of God and pulled under the weight of the absence of thought, spun out hard into the consuming bliss of total oblivion.

Once it was over, Piper sat still, trying to catch her breath, but her breath didn't want to be caught – sometimes it could be obnoxious. Chaz was still hard inside her. Her breath giggled and danced in front of her, taunting Piper while she franticly swung and snatched at it. Piper's breath jumped away from her flailing, grasping hands. Her breath noticed that Piper's face was starting to turn blue. The dancing breath felt bad. It realized that if Piper died it would have no place to live. Piper's unruly breath stopped dancing and stood still so its owner could catch it. Piper's hand swept down and snatched her breath and shoved it back into her mouth and sucked it down deep into her starving lungs.

Piper's chest heaved with renewed, deep breathing. She smiled with relief and looked over at Shelly. Her eyes ballooned with terror.

Shelly was moving in a deep trance, his eyes closed, his cock buried deep inside a wizened Gypsy woman, her saggy legs spread wide, naked on the table below him. Dust, flour, and powdered sugar rose off her wrinkled, age-ravaged skin each time Shelly thrust into her. Piper felt bile rise in her throat at the sight of Shelly pounding on the ancient woman.

Piper screamed at her oblivious boylyoyly. "Stop it, Shell! Get off that scraggly old Gypsy bitch!"

Shelly turned to Piper and blew her a kiss.

"I'm coming, Piper, I'm coming," he repeated in a flat, mocking monotone, his eyes dead and gray.

His body went rigid. Dust and sugar rose off the old woman as Shelly thrust into her one final time. Shelly glanced over his shoulder at Piper and then collapsed on top of the Gypsy crone.

Something moved under Piper. She looked down to a toothless, grime-covered Gypsy man with two glass eyes. The ancient man wiggled his cock inside her and winked.

Piper's throat rattled. Screams roared out of her mouth. She moved to pry herself off the Gypsy man but their thighs were melted together. Her gooey skin stretched when she pulled her body upward. She punched her upper thigh to try and jar her leg loose. Her fist sank deep into her flesh. Piper howled and yanked her arm. Her hand was stuck! Her legs were turning into dough!

Squirming and thrusting beneath her, the Gypsy man laughed menacingly and pressed his dirty fingers through her skin and into her thighs. Piper sank further as more and more of her pallid flesh turned into a sticky, sweet, wet dough.

Engulfed in panic and revulsion, Piper looked across the table at Shelly. Her faithful boylyboyly and the Gypsy woman were cooing at one another, embraced in the sweetness of afterglow. Shelly ran his fingers through the old woman's silver hair while she stroked his semi-erect knob with her crinkled hand. They smiled at each other and then gazed at Piper.

Shelly's cock started to grow and grow until it was a two-foot-long, six-inch-wide bulging shaft of flesh. He stood up on the pic-nick table bench and angled his new cock down at Piper's sinking chest.

Piper tried to swipe her hands out at Shelly's leering giggle stick but she no longer had hands, only fingerless wads of hand-shaped dough. The naked old Gypsy woman stood behind Shelly. She buried her face in his ass crack. Her wrinkled, flabby arms wound around Shelly.

With oversized 100% cotton oven mitts on both hands, the Gypsy lady jerked his massive man hose. Shelly started mumbling and flexing his arms. The muscles in his neck tightened.

Shelly screamed. "Oh, fork forkily forking fork, fork, FORK!!!!"

The magic Gypsy lady's busy mitt-covered hands threw him into the throes of an orgasm that was more insanely intense than anything Shelly had ever experienced or imagined or imagined that he could one day possibly imagine experiencing.

Saliva and chewed bits of tongue flew from Shelly's mouth. His eyes glowed bright red. His eyebrows burst into flames. Pitch-black smoke billowed from his anus and scorching hot grease shot out of his cock nozzle in a violent stream, shooting down onto Piper's soft, doughy skin.

Piper cried out in agony as the grease splashed onto her raw dough flesh. Bubbles appeared on her doughy thighs and arms. Her pale skin turned a crispy, golden brown.

Shelly rested a hand on his hip. A huge smile broke out across his face. Then he was laughing. Then the Gypsy lady was laughing. She peeked out from behind Shelly's ass, her face covered in soot, and laughed at Piper.

Piper shrieked. The searing, burning pain of being cooked alive obliterated all other sensations. Sweet partially hydrogenated corn syrup tears flowed down her melting face. Her head sank until her chin rested on her sticky dough chest. Hot grease splashed up onto her face and burned out her eyes.

Everything went dark. All Piper saw was black. All she felt was scorching agony. All she heard were the cries inside her head, growing louder and louder and louder and pushing inside her until there was a quick feeling of wind rushing through the pain. Something slapped hard against her forehead.

Starting awake, Piper opened her eyes to a vision of fuzzy green. Her body shook. She lugged her top half up off the solid surface and looked down at the faded green top of the picnic table.

An ominous wind blew through the food truck park. An empty cup rolled under the table and bumped into Shelly's shoe. Slowly, he looked up at Piper. She was staring straight ahead, breathing hard, rubbing her forehead, and crying. He rubbed his eyes and scanned their surroundings. The park was empty. Litter bounced and fluttered across the concrete, tossed around on the breeze. The uninterested high-mast lights gazed down on the lone couple.

Shelly turned around to look for the Gypsy food truck, only to see a blank space where the truck had been parked. Shelly's body was sore, especially his ass. He patted Piper's arm to get her attention.

"Piper...Piper."

She blinked her wide eyes and started screaming.

Shelly grabbed Piper's hands. "Piper, stop screaming, you'll wake the squirrels," he said.

Piper blinked again. Her eyes relaxed. "What?"

"You were screaming. Are you okay?"

"Oh, weird," Piper said, wringing her hands in embarrassment. "I hope I didn't wake the squirrels. They can be so violent when they get woken up all of a sudden like."

"Why were you screaming?" Shelly asked.

Piper ran her hands across her head and rubbed her eyes. "I don't know. I can't remember. My head hurts."

"I think we should go," Shelly said, looking around nervously. "We're the only ones here and I have an unexplainable pain in my ass."

"What time is it?" Piper asked.

Shelly pulled up his hoodie sleeve and checked his watch. "It's 11:33 pm."

"No, that's impossible."

"Check your phone."

Piper took her phone out of her hoodie pocket. She studied the screen, blinked twice, and looked up at Shelly. "Shnitt, mine says the same thing."

"It was 7:50 when I went to get the second funnel cake," Shelly said. "And I should know; I keep accurate track of time with my trusty Valkos brand wristwatch, now available in three stylish colors with authentic orphan skin wristbands."

"Piss on my shoe that is a sweet and surely reliable watch, but that doesn't answer my question. What the fork happened? Time doesn't just disappear like that."

"How the fork should I know, Piper," Shelly said, his voice rising with agitation.

"Hey, don't forking yell at me!" Piper said in a muted shout. She exhaled hard.

"Sorry. I'm just confused."

"It's okay Shell, I'm confused too," Piper placed a gentle hand on Shelly's arm. "Let's get outta here. This is forking creepy."

"Fork yeah it is," Shelly agreed.

With pain in their bodies and fear in their minds, Piper and Shelly scrambled off the benches and ventured into the night.

TWO. Wednesday Morning: Shelly's House, Breakfast

Piper had been staring at Shelly's ear from across the breakfast table for about three minutes and thirteen seconds straight.

She said, "There's something on your ear."

Piper reached over and ran her finger over the dry, bumpy, crusty, golden, shiny spot of skin that sat on top of Shelly's right ear looking like a cross between a scab and a piece of old, discarded funnel cake.

"What is it," Shelly asked, although part of him didn't want to know and the other part didn't care, but just wanted to eat his Valkos brand pale oats in silence.

"I don't know. Wait..."

Again, Piper slid her finger back and forth over the spot of crispy flesh on the top of Shelly's ear. Her brow creased in concentration. "It looks like crust. It feels like crust." Piper's eyes turned cold. Her eyebrows drew in. She pulled in a low gasp and whispered, "I think it's crust."

Shelly jerked back. "What!? There's no forking way I could have crust. I get my shots every year."

"Sometimes the shots don't work, Shell."

"No! I trust in my shots! They always work!" Shelly argued.

"Look, I'm just saying, don't worry, it's no big deal. Lots of people get the crusties. They take medicines and it goes away."

Shelly felt along the top of his ear. His fingers bumped over the small crusty area. Filled with alarm, he jumped up from the breakfast table and hurried to the bathroom. Leaning in close to the mirror and bending and inspecting, he stated the obvious:

"Oh no! Oh shnitt! I've got crust!"

Piper slinked into the bathroom doorway.

"Stop whining, it's gonna be fine. We'll get you to the doctor, you'll get some medicine, and it'll go away. Stop being so dramatic."

Shelly clenched fistfuls of hair. He spun in a semi-circle and did the locally recognized young person's dance of distress, which was developed by a core of rabid fans of the dinge pop group Harmony Lull. The dance was first seen outside of concert venues when it was announced that the show was sold out.

"We have to go now!" Shelly screeched, "Before it spreads. Crust always spreads!"

Piper rolled her eyes in disbelief. "For the sake of fork, forking calm the fork down!"

Shelly bulldozed his way out of the bathroom, shoving Piper into the hallway.

"I gotta find my Citizen's Medical information card that tells me who my doctor is and where they're located."

"You don't know who your doctor is?" Piper said. "Who doesn't know who their company-assigned doctor is?"

Ignoring her, Shelly sped into his bedroom. He frantically rifled and tossed and ransacked and scoured until his desk drawers and their contents were strewn all around. While Piper looked on in silence, Shelly crawled along his bedroom floor, searching through the mess, all the while mumbling curses under his breath until he seized upon a small object in the clutter.

Shelly held up a small, laminated rectangular piece of paper. "Ha! All Chaz Luger imitators can suck it! I found my card!" He stood up in triumph. "Yes! That's right! Now, where's my forking phone?"

With a roll of her eyes, Piper slouched back to the kitchen table and picked up Shelly's phone. Her voice echoed through the hall. "It's right here."

Piper strolled back into Shelly's room and held out his Smarty Phone. "Now, will you calm down?"

Shelly's eyes grew wide. He kicked the wall and screamed, "I've forking got forking crust! Don't you forking tell me to forking calm down! Fork!!!!"

He snatched the phone from Piper. Holding the card in his trembling hand, Shelly scanned the digits and dialed the number. The line rang on the other end. He waited.

"If this is such an emergency, and if you're so freaked out, shouldn't you just go to the hospital?" Piper asked.

"No!" Shelly snapped, "Hospitals suck, I hate them!"

Piper leaned up against the doorframe. She ran a hand over her face and then stared into the carpet, hoping to see something that would distract her from this annoying situation.

Shelly held the phone close to his ear, his tense, gripping fingers turning white at the tips. He held his breath. After seventeen rings a nurse picked up on the other end.

"Good morning. Thank you for calling Happy Get-Well Health Center #1408, a Valkos brand medical station. This is Nurse Sheena; how may I help you?"

"Um, yes, I need to please make an appointment to see..." Shelly's eyes skipped across the information card in his hand, "...the honorable Dr. Morris Norris. I need to see him as soon as possible, please. It's super urgent, like, for real."

"And what do you need to see the doctor about today?" Nurse Sheena asked in a sing-song voice.

Shelly paused and exhaled.

"I think I have the crust," he said. His voice was low and dejected. He looked at Piper, who stood still and silent, her eyes fixed on the floor.

"Well, let's see here. Why don't you come on in at 1:23 this afternoon?"

"I like that number, Nurse Sheena, it's very specific, but are you sure you don't have anything earlier than that?" Shelly rocked back and forth from one foot to the other. Worry lines grew across his brow. "This is totally super urgent, for real."

"I understand sweetie, but that's the earliest we have. Our esteemed doctor is quite in demand these days," Nurse Sheena explained.

Shelly shook his head. The phone line crackled. "So, 1:23 then? Okay, I'll be there."

Piper was still staring at the carpet while Shelly rambled off his patient ID number and other pertinent information to the nurse before thanking her and saying bye. Shelly hit the end call button and turned to Piper. His eyes held tears that teetered on the edges of his eyes, threatening to spill out and rush down his cheeks.

"Assholes to Allah, this is unbelievable! The doctor can't see me for another three hours!" Shelly shouted. "What the fork is wrong with him!? What the fork is this!? I have crust! I have forking crust!!"

Piper backed out into the hall, stepping away from Shelly's deafening whine.

"Alright, first of all, quit acting like that shrill, orphan robot from the Scoscar-winning film, *The Trials of Little Bitch*. Second, I say yet again -calm the fork down, it's only three hours."

"Three hours?! The crust can spread super crazy fast! Don't they know that?!"

"I know, but you're gonna be fine. You just need to relax, for real. Getting upset makes it worse. You know crust is a living organism that responds to negative emotions."

"But-?!"

"Shut it! That's enough!" Piper's tone was stern and commanding.

Shelly gave up. "Fine." His voice wound down to a self-pitying whimper. "I'm gonna go watch a story on my fun box." He slinked away, sullen and mumbling to himself. "How did I get crust? How could this happen to me?"

Feeling helpless and annoyed, Piper lowered her eyes to the floor and walked back to the kitchen.

THREE. Three Hours Later, The Doctor's Office

The honorable Dr. Morris Norris leaned in close, swiping the light of his otoscope back and forth over the top of Shelly's right ear. The doctor stood on a stepstool so that his crotch hovered mere inches from Shelly's face.

Piper sat in a plastic chair beside the examining table. Her eyes bounced around the bland, clinical space, where everything was painted different shades of beige and for some reason, a decomposing bunch of bananas sat on a counter across the room. *Maybe that's his lunch*, Piper mused.

Gray and black mold grew on the once-white drop-down ceiling. Yellow and pink stains littered the dirty white tile floor. Old tinfoil ashtrays sat on counters and inside doorless cabinets around the room. Piper counted them. There were eleven. A faded promotional poster for the Valkos brand male-enhancement drug Titanium Dick Erectors caught her eye. She smiled and stifled a laugh. Feeling the cold of the room, Piper pulled her hoodie close around her thin body and crossed her legs tight, the whispers of her orange corduroys loud in the ultra-quiet space.

The doctor turned off the otoscope and stood up straight, raising himself to the fullness of his short, stumpy height, pushing his crotch even closer to Shelly's face. Shelly scooted away. The doctor passed a hand over his buzzed, brown hair, stopping at the top of his head and scratching.

"Yep, you forked up son," the doctor said to Shelly. "You got that crust."

"No shnitt, doctor," Shelly snapped, "I already knew that. That's why I'm here; I want you to get rid of it!"

Dr. Morris Norris stepped back. "Hey, whoa now! No need to get aggressive, son. I'm gonna give you some medicines that's gonna clear your shnitt right up, gonna take that crust right off."

Doctor Morris Norris sat the otoscope down, stepped off his stool, and reached for the prescription pad in his front coat pocket. He gave Piper a lusty glance.

"Damn, son; this your girlyirly?"

"Yeah... So?"

"She been up in here this whole time?"

"Yeah."

Dr. Norris turned and fully faced Piper, picking at her with deviant eyes. "Damn! She forking fine as hell. I'd tear that bajingo up!"

Piper blushed and giggled. "Thank you, Doctor," she said, her eyelids fluttering.

Dr. Norris's nostrils flared. His eyes bulged. His creamy orange skin flashed a wave of red. He shouted, "Bitch, did I say you could speak?"

His words deflated Piper's happy bubble. Taken aback, she stammered, "N-n-no..."

Dr. Norris shook his head from side to side. He stomped on the floor with his mucky sneakers and his hefty belly jiggled. He squealed and ran to the counter on the other side of the room. The doctor franticly grabbed at the bunch of rotting bananas that sat near the sink and tore one off.

"Who bananas these is?" Morris Norris yelled.

Shelly looked at the doctor and shrugged his shoulders.

"What?" Piper asked in confusion.

"Bitch, was I talkin' to you?" Dr. Norris shot back.

"I don't know who you were talking to," Piper said. "I have no idea what's going on."

Dr. Norris huffed and peeled the nearly black banana. "Shnitt, I'll tell you what the fork is goin' on. I'm gonna give this here nilla his 'scrimption. Then y'all's gonna get the fork up outta my office." Dr. Morris Norris stopped and leered at Piper. "But you can come back anytime, baby."

Piper blushed.

The doctor spun around and thrust a scribbled prescription out to Shelly. He bit off half the gray banana in one bite. "Thems is pills. Take them shnitts and call me in two days," he shouted at Shelly, bits of banana flying onto Shelly as he spoke.

Shelly grabbed the small square of paper that hopefully held the key to his cure and backed away from the banana projectiles. "Okay, doctor, thanks."

"Now," Dr. Morris screamed, "skee-dat mutha-forkas! Gets the fork up out my face, I got shnitt to do." The doctor turned away from Piper and Shelly, crossed the room, and stood in the corner, munching on the banana and singing under his breath.

Without another word, Piper and Shelly left the examining room and went to the front desk to pay the bill.

· · · ·

FOUR. Five Minutes Later, Piper's Car

Shelly fidgeted in the passenger seat, unable to get comfortable.

"I thought Valkos brand doctors were supposed to be good," he said. He stared out the window in a daze.

Piper steered the car out onto the main road. "They're the only doctors unless you want to go to the dark medicine doctor in West Mable Town. And you heard about what happened to that one woman who went there; the one with the axe, remember? Besides, I don't know, he seemed okay to me."

Shelly exploded. "What!? Are you insane!? He's completely incompetent! He barely examined me! And... and... why did he keep using the 'N' word with us? It's rude! I think he's racist." Shelly picked at the crust on his right ear. "He had that orangish skin tone. He must be a creamy, which explains the leering, the overt sexuality, the disrespect, the racism."

"He only said the 'N' word once, Shell. And besides, why do you always have to bring race into everything? We're nillas and he's a creamy, who forking cares? I thought he was sweet."

Shelly's eyes rolled in irritated circles. "Sweet? Sweet?! He was-"

Piper cut in. Pink sparks flew from her eyes and danced around the car. "Hey! Stop being so forking judgey! And quit snapping at me! You're just mad because he was into me."

"You liked it!" Shelly roared.

Piper's eyes began to glow. "No shnitt I liked it! Who doesn't like compliments, Shelly?"

"Compliments? Compliments?!" Shelly shouted. "He was incredibly disrespectful! He called you the 'B' curse! I don't... I can't... It's not..." At a loss, he shook his head and rubbed his eyes. A low gurgle sounded from the back of his throat and he shook with violence until, after two minutes and eighteen-sevenths of a second had passed, Shelly became very, very still and quiet.

The bright pink glow in Piper's eyes became a soft, sad yellow.

"I just don't understand why you're so mad about someone saying they like how I look. You never say it. And that hurts, Shelly, it forking hurts."

Shelly turned to Piper and spoke softly. "I'm sorry, you're right. There's nothing wrong with compliments, even if they're coming from a doctor. I'm sorry I snapped at you. It's just the crust. It's already starting to get to me. Just take me home, please."

Piper exhaled hard. "Okay, whatever."

Piper clicked on her blinker to take the next left into Shelly's neighborhood. Her sad, yellow eyes began to glow pink again. *He just doesn't forking get it*, she thought. *He never tells me that I turn him on, or that he even likes the extra layer of grease I add to my hair, or my shoe holes, or anything! Fork!*

The small car rolled to a stop in front of Shelly's house.

Shelly leaned over and lighted a kiss on Piper's cheek. "Thanks for driving me, Piper."

Piper nodded and faked a smile while the pink blazed in her pupils. Shelly leaned back, opened the door, and stepped out.

"See you tomorrow?" Shelly asked.

"Maybe," Piper said, looking straight ahead.

Shelly's shoulders slumped. "Okay... well, bye."

"Bye," Piper replied, her gaze still fixed straight ahead.

After Shelly shut the car door, Piper turned and watched him shuffle up the driveway to his house. Once he was out of sight, she drove away with pink fires burning in her eyes.

FIVE. The Next Day, Piper's House

Piper decided to ignore Shelly's calls. She was still hurt and angry with him for how he'd spoken to her on the way home from the doctor's office. He couldn't be such a whiny little twit and get away with it. And he had been rude and unappreciative of her as a girlyirly. Why couldn't he share in her joy of receiving leers and compliments? Like, what the actual hell?

When her phone wouldn't stop ringing because Shelly wouldn't stop calling, Piper turned the phone off and put it to rest under her pillow. Then she left the house. For at least twenty-two seconds Piper was consumed with intense separation anxiety, but, as she drove through town, a great sense of peace and freedom filled her soul.

"Wow, so this is what going phoneless feels like!" She bellowed in the empty car. "This is amazing!"

Back in Piper's room, beneath her soft, hair-grease-coated pillow, the tired cell phone sighed and relaxed and thought to itself, *I hope that bitch don't never come back.*

And then the phone decided to take a nap while it still had the chance because the life of a phone is uncertain and one might never know when one might get smashed, dropped in a toilet, or shoved up someone's rectum and smuggled into an adult re-programming facility to be used to take unscrupulous, blackmail oriented photographs and make unauthorized calls to relatives who aren't happy to hear from their sad and lonely, incarcerated step-cousins. Truly, you never knew. One just had to take advantage of opportunities when they presented themselves.

Over dinner that evening, Piper's mom asked her about her day. She told her mom that she'd spent the afternoon at Captivity Playhouse, wrestling with bears, which wasn't true at all. Lying to her mother stung Piper's heart, but she knew her mother disapproved of her Chaz Luger fixation: Piper's mom hated the fact that her daughter's obsession so closely rivaled her own. The thought of Piper hiding out at the West Mable Town Mall's News and Information Kiosk all day pouring over stats and researching would throw her mother into a fit of rage, just like it had done on that fateful Saturday morning not so long ago. *

(*Narrator's Note: Although I have done my utmost to include all pertinent dates and times in the retelling of this narrative, neither Piper nor her mother were able to recall the exact date of this incident. The editors and I assume this is due to the trauma involved with both parties. Please excuse this vagary. We hope that it does not detract from your enjoyment of this tale. Thank you for your understanding.)

• • • •

PIPER HAD BEEN AT THE breakfast table tearing into a bowl of Zonger O's and watching Chaz Luger's debut feature film, iconic erotic writer/filmmaker Mandy De Sandra's renowned classic, *Friday Night Fuckfest in F Minor*, a somber tale about a smooth jazz musician, "Blondie" Phelps Martini, who contracts an incurable STD from a female tuba player that causes his fingers to turn into penises. His penis fingers make him the smoothest saxophone player of all time. The fame and glory that comes along with finger penises and ultimate saxophone jazziness proves to be too much for the young star and he falls into the familiar trappings of drugs, booze, and lewd gesturing.

Things take a downward turn when the musician is kidnapped by East Mable Town mob boss Princess Lai Me and forced to perform smooth jazz gigs and sexy antics for the mobster and her vast harem of female servants. The film climaxes with a fork-for-freedom showdown between Phelps and the Princess, who has never had an orgasm in her life. If Phelps can bring the princess to climax, then she will set him free. In a stunning, action-packed, forty-minute scene of non-stop sexiness that culminates with Princess Lai Me dying from a heart attack caused by 37 consecutive orgasms, Phelps proves that even a legendary mob boss is no match for penis fingers. He is victorious and the Princess's harem is set free, only to worry about where they will live and work now that their boss is dead and they have no skills or formal training in any area. It is a bittersweet, tender, and moving ending that always brings tears to the eyes of even the most cynical viewers.

With its mixture of brooding comedy, sensuality, and anal antics -plus a super smooth musical score by the veteran composer Dick Mayhem- the film was a smash with critics and fans alike, rocketing Chaz Luger into instant stardom, making him a household name and the object of lust of undersexed housewives as well as young women and their middle-aged mothers throughout Mable Town.

· · · ·

ON THAT MORNING, AS Piper crunched on her cereal with her eyes glued to the screen of the small TV on the table, her mom walked in to get some coffee. Passing by Piper, she glanced at the TV.

"Now, there's a good way to start the day," she said with a smile.

"Sshhhh, Mom! I'm trying to watch my favorite movie," Piper snapped. She leaned in closer to the TV and turned the volume up.

Piper's mom poured some coffee. "How many times have you seen it?"

Piper turned to her mother, her mouth full of the sugary sweet O's, and shot her a scathing look. She moved her eyes back to the screen. "It'll be forty-three times after this one."

Piper's mom chuckled and she sat down at the table. She took a sip of her hot, black coffee.

"I've seen it sixty-seven times. I know Chaz's monologue from the second act, where he's drunk and high on glue, yelling at his penis fingers, by heart," Piper's mom bragged.

"Maybe you know the words, but you don't know what they mean. You don't know the *feeling*," Piper snarled.

"I do so know the feeling!" Her mom retorted. "I know Chaz's heart! You didn't know me before I became the one you call 'mom'; when I was troubled and filled with the recklessness of youth! He played that part just for me!"

"Shut up, Mom! He played that part for me, not you! And I know it, like for real, okay!"

Piper's mom gripped her coffee mug. "What do you know, huh? You're just a twenty-two-year-old little girlyirly with barely any life to speak of!"

A pink glow simmered behind Piper's eyes. She lowered her spoon into her cereal. She spoke quietly and slowly. "I am not a forking little girlyirly, mother. And I know that Chaz wants someone young and hot and greasy, like me, only me, not some old sass-bag like you, that's what the fork I know."

"How dare you!" Piper's mom hissed. "Chaz is a man who values experience and refinement in a lover! He doesn't want some young floozy who doesn't know her way around a man, a real man that is!"

"You can never have him! He's mine!" Piper screamed, slamming her fist down on the table, pink light filling her eyes. "And I wrote him seventeen lust letters with my menstrual blood and sent them all first-class mail and I know that any day now, any forking day, he's going to write me back and then we're going to be together!"

"No! He'll never be yours, you two-bit hussy!" Piper's mom shouted. "You're spelling is so bad it's offensive and you write like a blind goat who never passed basic grammar!"

Piper's eyes ballooned to four times their original size and glowed hot, neon pink. She threw back her head and roared. "AAAAHHHHH!! I forking hate you! I—"

Piper's mom leaped up and poured the cup of steaming hot coffee into her daughter's open mouth, stifling her screams. Piper fell out of her chair clutching her throat. Hot pink lasers shot out of her eyes. Piper's mom threw her hands over her face. Piper pulled herself to her feet, filling the kitchen with the blinding pink light. She grabbed her half-eaten bowl of Zonger O's and hurled at it her mother. The bowl nailed her mom in the chest. She stumbled back and crashed into the stove.

Piper's mom reached across the stove and grasped the handle of a cast iron skillet. With one hand shielding her eyes and the other on the skillet handle, she attacked Piper, lunging and swinging the heavy pan. Piper dodged the flying skillet. She spun and her mom swung again. This time Piper miscalculated. The skillet hammered her on the shoulder and sent her flying onto the table. Piper lay across the table on her stomach, groaning in pain while her mother struggled to breathe.

"Piper, dear," her mother said, panting, "in the end, Chaz will only be able to have one of us, and it's not going to be you."

Piper felt a surging pain in her chest as her mother's words cut into her. Sorrowful tears of rage filled Piper's eyes, crystalizing the lasers and turning them into solid beams that burned holes through the tabletop.

She stood up and spun toward her mother, her pink lasers blowing out the kitchen window and killing the wall clock. Piper's mom brought the iron skillet up to shield her face. The lasers struck the metal and bounced up into the ceiling. Without thinking, Piper looked up, following the bouncing lasers. Her eyes traced lines over the ceiling. There was a loud crack. The ceiling began to cave in. A wooden support beam fell toward her mother. Piper leaped and pushed her out of the way just before the beam crashed down on the kitchen floor right where she had been standing.

After the falling beam almost crushed her mother, Piper's anger turned to fear and worry. She grabbed her mom and pulled her down. They crouched together under the kitchen table while sheetrock and wood crashed down all around them. Huddled together, they held each other.

When the debris stopped falling, they heard the voice of their favorite adult star coming through from the small TV above their heads. The film was still on. It was the heartbreaking closing scene. Phelps Martini was setting the Princess's harem free. Piper and her mother looked into one another's eyes and recited Chaz's lines along with him:

"Go now, gentle sluts. You are free from the tyranny of the Princess! Free to laugh, free to live ... free to love!"

And as "Blondie" Phelps Martini played his smooth saxophone on a mountaintop while the credits rolled, Piper and her mother wept in each other's arms.

"Oh Piper, I'm so sorry!" Her mom wailed.

"I'm sorry too, mom!" Piper cried.

"From this day onward, even though I know in my heart that I and only I will ever be the one for Chaz Luger and that you will never spread your skinny legs for his majestic love thruster and that our rivalry will stand eternal, I promise to never again fight with you over him and to live in peace, harmony, and mother daughterly love from now on," her mother said.

Piper sniffled and nodded. "Okay, Mom, that's cool."

Then they hugged for two more minutes before Piper's mom insisted that they get out from under the table and call a local contractor to come out and appraise the damage.

But that was then, and, even though they had made peace, Piper thought it would be better to lie about what she'd been doing rather than risk another fight which would invariably result in having to call out the contractors- the dirty, dirty contractors with their tight shirts, low hanging jeans, and bulging crotches.

Piper's mother sighed. Her shoulders sagged. She mumbled something about her daughter's choice of recreational activities.

"It's safe Mom. The bears are partially sedated. Look, I didn't even get any cuts this time." Piper held out her arms for her mother to inspect.

Her mother gave a disapproving look. "It's not fair to the bears. It's not nice. They shouldn't be treated like toys."

After some conversation, they agreed that bears probably don't enjoy wrestling with humans as much as one might think.

• • • •

AFTER DINNER, PIPER helped her mom with the cleanup, during which they engaged in a spirited debate over the sensitive topic of Ninja prostitution and enslavement. Since Piper was a Ninja rights activist, her mom liked to pick arguments with her on the subject, even though she never revealed which side she was on. Piper had discovered that most people felt like her mother pretended to feel, and had no apparent sympathy for the plight of the Ninja.

This shocked and saddened Piper, who thought it was totally whack that people would use Ninjas for their sexual pleasure and then, sixteen minutes later, deny them the right to share the cab ride home and force them to use the Ninja tricycle rideshare program, the most prejudice rideshare program ever devised. Piper couldn't understand how such a great, wise, and sexy people could be treated so awfully.

For hundreds and thousands of years, Ninja men were revered for their super-rad sex powers, sleek fashion sense, and the ability to walk through walls. Ninja women were praised for their intellect, jumping skills, and mad tight boobies. Even Ninja children were held in high esteem for their comedic stylings and mad-cap shenanigans. It is spoken in town legends, and recorded in Levon Shivers' massive tome, *Mable Town: History and Lore*, that Ninjas once governed the quaint burg.

Despite their unparalleled fighting abilities, the Ninjas are a kind and peaceful people and the township prospered under their reign. But there was another group who wanted control. They couldn't stand that nice people were in charge and making positive decisions that were good for all citizens. These evil-minded schemers were called the Baptists, and they never knew when to leave well enough alone, or even understood what the fork that old saying meant.

Through their spies that were embedded deep within the Ninja community, the Baptists learned that by watching *American Ninjas in Heat Part 17* backward, all the Ninja secrets would be revealed. With this method, the Baptist leaders discovered the Ninjas' one fatal weakness: tater tots.

One summer evening the Baptist revolutionaries opened a tater tot stand right in front of the Ninjas' lair. They fried the delectable tots day and night, the irresistible fumes rising and drifting into the Ninjas' home.

The Ninja men, women, and tiny Ninja babies did all they could to resist, even going as far as closing their windows to shield themselves from the deadly aroma, but, alas, the pull of the tots was too strong and one morning the Ninjas all stormed out of their hideout and bum rushed the tater tot stand. Within hours every man, woman, and Ninja child was lying on the ground, their bellies full and bulging. Tears streamed down their faces as they cried out in regret, their powers gone, while the Baptists cackled with glee.

"Mable Town is ours!" The Baptists shouted. "And lo, verily we say unto you, let us enslave the Ninja peoples for our pleasure and let us make homogenous idols and strip malls, and lo, let everything be bland!"

And so it was that the Baptists took over the town.

Later on, that same day, an investigative report of high moral repute revealed that the Baptist husbands were pissed that the single Ninja men had been satisfying the Baptist wives on the down low for centuries with their unrivaled boners and skills of total sexiness and that this was the main reason why the Baptists sabotaged the Ninja government.

Following the revolution, the Baptists kept the Ninjas sedated by keeping them hooked on the tots. The sleekest and strongest Ninja men were sold off into prostitution. They became dependent on Titanium Dick Erectors, the flagship product of the Baptists' new corporation, Valkos Enterprises, which their tater tot habit required them to use to be able to perform. The Ninja children were placed in cigarette rolling factories and forced laughter sitcoms while their heartbroken mothers were put into harsh thinking camps where their prized intellects were scoured and their advanced ideas were harvested, reformatted, and used to make new and deadly weapons to protect the Baptists' corporation.

It made Piper sick that this was how the world worked. She couldn't understand what she regarded as her mother's refusal to see things as they were.

"Piper, you aren't going to change my mind," Piper's mom said. "Ninjas are different. They deserve to be slaves. Now, if you'll excuse me, I need to get to bed."

"Mom, that doesn't explain anything. You're not giving me a reason."

Piper's mom ignored her words, kissed her on the cheek, and grinned. "I do appreciate your help with the dishes."

"I forking help you with the dishes every night, Mom. Now, forking tells me why you hate Ninjas!"

Piper stood in front of her mom, her legs apart, her arms folded over her chest, blocking the doorway. Her mom made a meek attempt to push by.

"No, Mom, you're not going anywhere until you tell me what the fork your beef is with Ninjas! I wanna know and I wanna know right forking now!"

Piper's mom shuffled her feet. "Sweetie, I really do need to get to bed..."

"No, Mom!" Piper shouted. "I want the truth and I want it now!"

Piper angled her eyes at her mom. Her pupils began to give off the familiar pink glow. Piper's mom started running in place. Her eyes darted over Piper's shoulder and into the hallway.

"Mom!" Piper yelled.

"No, I won't tell!"

"Ha! So, there is a reason!" Piper screamed as her eyes glowed brighter.

Piper's mother shielded her face with a forearm and ran faster in place, her breasts bouncing as her pace increased.

"No, Piper! I won't reveal the reason behind my disdain for Ninjas which also holds the secret to *your* superpowers!"

Piper's pink eyes exploded with fury, bathing the dim kitchen with blinding pink light and heat. Piper's mom cried out and pressed both hands tight over her eyes.

Piper screamed: "Lula Brianna Lee! You will tell me now!"

Piper had called her mother by her full name. Lula knew that shnitt had just gotten really real, like, for real.

Lula shook her head side to side, tossing her shaggy light brown hair around on her head. She pumped her legs harder and her feet went faster and faster until they turned into a swirling, circular blur. Lines of distress grew across her forehead.

"I love you, Piper!" Lula shouted. "You were such a nice girlyirly before you got hooked on those Gypsy funnel cakes! I should have warned you about your possible genetic predisposition to food addiction! I'm sorry, Piper! I'm so sorry!"

"Tell! Me! NOW!" Piper boomed, leaning into her mom's face, her breath blowing her mom's hair back.

"Your father is a Ninja!" Lula cried out. "Ours was a forbidden love because I was a Baptist. He had a penis of steel, a mind of fury, and a heart of jelly. I lost him to his tater tot addiction and I'll never forgive him! He was my one true love and he chose fried yummy goodness over me!"

Tears poured out from behind Lula's hands as she screamed out her confession. Her spinning feet lifted her off the ground. She hovered in front of her stunned daughter, bawling.

"Good night, Piper, sleep tight! I Love you!"

Lula's feet connected with the floor. High-pitched screeches filled the room. A cloud of smoke rose behind her as she tore a streak across the cheap linoleum floor and sped out of the kitchen, slamming into Piper and sending her bewildered daughter flying out of the doorway and tumbling down the hall. Piper flipped and landed upside down against a wall. The pink heat faded from her eyes.

"Love you too, mom!" Piper called out.

Piper turned over and sat against the wall.

"Wow, my dad's a forking Ninja!" She whispered to herself with excitement. "I wonder if I can walk through walls."

Piper sat and thought until her body went numb. Then she got up and went to bed.

The day was over and no one knew where Shelly went or didn't go or what he did or didn't do because no one cared to ask. This made Piper a tiny bit sad so before she fell asleep, she turned her phone back on just in case he might call.

Six. Early the Next Morning, Piper's Room

Piper was enjoying some quality alone time with the Luger 9000 Deluxe Automatic, the world's first thought-activated dildo made from the flesh of dead adult film stars whom Chaz Luger had defeated in pay-per-view Fork to The Death competitions when her Smarty Phone rang.

"No, no, no! Not now!" She called out in between groans. She gripped the sheets. The Luger 9000 pounded into her.

The call went to voice mail just as she started to cum. Piper's orgasm lifted her above the dull reality of her life and into the beautiful, into the realm of the true and the possible. Everything made sense. Time was suspended and her flesh collided with the pure essence of the universe. She saw it all and then it was gone. It was over. And her phone was ringing.

Piper turned off the Luger 9000 and put the life-size member into her mouth. Running her fingers over her clit and in and out of her hot, wet lady box, she moved the toy in and out of her mouth. Once she felt cooled down, she put the beloved 9000 Deluxe Automatic back into its silk-lined case, stashed it in the bottom drawer of her nightstand, and collapsed on her bed, rubbing her breasts and basking in the afterglow. And once again her phone began to ring.

With her chest heaving and her fingers glistening she grabbed the phone and answered it on the second ring.

"Hello," she said, still breathing heavily.

"Hey, it's me," Shelly said. He paused. "What are you doing? You're all out of breath."

"Chaz Luger's been nailing me in the ass for the last half hour."

"No way! You're flexin'!"

"Yeah, I just ran up the stairs to get my phone," she lied.

"Oh..." Shelly replied.

"How are you today? How's the crust?" Piper asked.

There was a short silence. Shelly cleared his throat. "It's worse," he said.

"Call the prophets! Is it worse? Like, how?"

Piper rolled over and took a deep whiff of her wet fingers. She shuddered with wonder and smiled wide.

"My entire right ear is covered with crust and it's grown over most of the right side of my head and neck too," Shelly explained.

"Oh no... Shells-," Piper began before Shelly cut back in.

"I called the doctor's office like I was supposed to. They want me to come in this afternoon."

Piper fell silent. Her wide smile faded. Dull reality pressed in on her.

"Can you take me?" Shelly asked.

"Of course," Piper answered. "What time is the appointment?"

"It's at two."

"I'll be at your house at one thirty. Okay?" Piper said.

"Okay. See you then. Bye."

"Bye sweetie, see you soon."

Piper pressed the end call button. Her mind floated away and she didn't try to stop it or reel it back in. She looked at the clock on her nightstand. It was only 8:45 a.m. She knew she had time for another round with the Luger 9000.

As she slid the mammoth, built-to-scale self-love toy inside her, her brain turned to fire and she broke into song:

Oh Chaz, my love to thee, praise Allah for cocks and bombs!
Oh Chaz, my love-to-be, take my life and heart and thumbs!

As she sang and the 9000 worked its magic, Piper was carried away into a mystical land of pleasure deep inside her 3rd mind.

Before Piper knew it, it was 11:42 a.m. and her pink polka dot sheets were soaked in sweet, sweet lady cum, sweat, and blood. She smiled at her mess and felt good about being such an enthusiastic young woman. Then she got up and skipped to the shower.

Seven. Later That Day, 1:32 To Be Exact, Shelly's House

Piper couldn't believe it. The crust had grown from a barely visible patch on the top of Shelly's right ear to spread and cover most of the right side of his head and neck. From what Shelly had described on the phone, it seemed to have spread even more since they'd talked that morning. The crust had covered his right eye and was encroaching on the right side of his mouth.

"Assholes to Allah, this is insane! Are you okay Shell?" Piper asked.

Shelly glared at her from his good eye, fuming in silence.

"Oh, yeah, I guess that was a stupid question... sorry," Piper said, lowering her eyes.

"Let's go," Shelly said in a cold and biting tone, pulling the hood of his sweatshirt up over his head and walking out the front door.

Piper popped her knuckles and put her hands on her hips. She shook her head. *That boy needs to check his forking attitude,* she thought as she stood in the doorway and watched him walk toward her car. Shelly reached the car and turned around.

"Come on Piper!" He yelled.

Piper's hands dropped from her hips and balled into fists. Her eyes began to glow.

"Fork!" she muttered under her breath, stomping out of the house and slamming the door behind her.

. . . .

EIGHT. Piper's car

After a few minutes of cruel quiet, Shelly mumbled a half-hearted apology. "I'm sorry I was rude to you back there. I'm just really freaking out. And I mean, really, I'm like, totally freaking the fork out."

Piper frowned. She felt bad for getting mad at him. She knew this must be totally forking scary for him. Her eyebrows crinkled in empathy. She rubbed Shelly's leg. "I know baby, I would be too, like for real, like totally. Don't worry about it, okay?"

"Okay". Shelly's eyes teared up. He started to sniffle. Piper looked over at him.

"Shell?" Piper began.

"I like you Piper... (Sniffle, sniffle) ...I like you so much! (Weird crying sound) ...if you had a dick, I'd suck it... I'd suck that shnitt so hard! I'd suck it so forking tight! That's how much... how much... I... I... (pulling back) ... that's how much I really, totally like you, for real."

Shelly sniffled and wiped his left eye. He smiled meekly at Piper, who was beaming with the pure light of total adoration.

"Flex? You'd suck it forking hard like, forking tight, for reals?"

"Totally!"

"Oh Shell, that's amazing, no one's ever said that to me before." Piper paused and looked deep into the dismal abyss of Shelly's good left eye. "I really like you, Shells, like- really for reals. If you had a hot, hairy whisker biscuit, I'd eat that shnitt. I'd eat it raw and slick." She rolled her tongue out and over her lips in the poise of a seductress.

Shelly felt his face flush hot and red. A billion pins pricked against his skin. He pulled them all out and tossed them out the window. The billions of pins punctured the tires of oncoming vehicles. Since they were traveling on a major road, this caused a massive pile-up, which resulted in two broken pinky fingers. The injured motorists were rushed to the hospital where they were chastised for not being more responsible and then executed because they had no pinky finger insurance.

Shelly pushed his feet down hard on the floorboard.

"Good fork! I'm getting all balled up all tight like. I can't get balled up like this, like, not now!" Shelly cried out. He stomped on the floorboard, slammed his head on the dash, and punched himself in the dick.

"AAAAHHHHHH!" He screamed as if it was the end of the world and he was the only person still alive and he had a case of blue balls that was ten-jillion times worse than any case of blue balls that any man in history had ever had, like, ever.

Shelly squirmed and writhed in agony, struggling with the automatic window controls on Piper's car like a two-fingered epileptic prostitute giving a hand job during a seizure.

The window came down just in time for Shelly to spew his breakfast of split pea soup, cream corn, hard-boiled eggs, sardines, tuna, pork brains in milk gravy, a pickle juice concentrate and sour cream float, and chocolate bars, all over the side of Piper's car. The rancid tang of fresh vomit wafted through the compact car, intoxicating Piper. Her super lady love muffin burned with desire, sending clouds of gray smoke billowing up from her crotch.

"Holy forking shnitt tits, Piper! You're on fire!" Shelly yelled.

Piper made some kind of garbled prehistoric cavewoman sound as lusty drool poured out of her mouth. She put the car on auto-drive. Seconds later Shelly's cock was in the warm wet of Piper's mouth. Shelly had never seen her like this. If only he'd known, he would've thrown up all the time.

His good eye rolled back in his head as Piper went up and down on his rock-hard joy stick, stopping to swirl and tease his head before going back down, all the way down, taking his full length into her mouth and down her throat, testing her gag reflex. The car puttered along the city streets while Piper's lips glided up and down Shelly's thick shaft, both car and lips bringing the passenger closer to his destination.

"Oh... oh... oh... shnitt on a pancake," Shelly mumbled.

Piper sped up, her lips and tongue going wild, her free hand massaging Shelly's balls. Shelly gripped the seat. His back stiffened.

"Oh... Piper... Oh, oh, oh Piper... Piper... Piper..."

The car turned itself into the doctor's office parking lot and headed for an empty spot near the front door.

"Piper... Piper... Oh... Ohhhhh..."

The car skidded to a stop. Shelly's hips thrust upward.

"PIPER!" Shelly called out as he exploded into his girlyirly's hot, salivating mouth.

Piper slurped and moaned in ecstasy as she swallowed every bit of Shelly's steaming man sauce until he was empty.

Shelly leaned back on the headrest, panting. He wiped a stray piece of corn off his cheek, accidentally knocking it into Piper's hair.

Piper sat up. Out of breath, she shuddered with delight. "Now that's how you drive a forking car!"

"Shnitt yeah!" Shelly agreed.

Piper looked at the dashboard clock. She wiped her hand across her mouth and licked her fingers. "I guess we should go in," she said.

"Okay, let's go."

Shelly and Piper got out of the car and went to see the doctor, hoping for the best but thinking of what they should have for lunch after the appointment was over.

Piper grabbed Shelly's ass when they passed through the door. She whispered in his ear. "Your cum tasted like sugar glaze. It was forking delicious."

Shelly smiled and for a second, he almost thought he would laugh.

NINE. A Few Minutes Later

The honorable Dr. Morris Norris chipped at the crust on Shelly's neck with a scalpel. Holding a magnifying glass with his other hand, he leaned in closer to inspect.

"Shnitt," Dr. Norris said, shaking his head and setting the magnifying glass down on the nearby counter. "I ain't never seen no crust like this befo'".

"What kind of crust do you think it is?" Shelly asked.

"How the fork should I know? Ain't, you listenin', nilla? I just said: 'I ain't never seen no crust like this befo'. Now, don't asks me no mo' questions and make me damn quote myself and shnitt. Damn!"

"Sorry" Shelly mumbled.

"Shnitt... now shut the fork up and hold still."

Dr. Norris waved the scalpel over Shelly's right cheek. He stopped near Shelly's ear, dug the knife in, and cut off a quarter-size chunk of the crust. Piper and Shelly watched the doctor hold the chunk of crust under his nose, inhale deeply, and then, with no hesitation, pop it in his mouth and begin to chew.

Piper and Shelly recoiled in revulsion and shock. As Dr. Norris chewed, an expression of deep contemplation spread across his face.

"Damn son," he said, spitting crumbs from his full mouth as he spoke, "this crust tastes like a damn funnel cake. You been eatin' them Gypsy funnel cakes? Huh?"

Shelly nodded. "Yeah, we ate some on Tuesday."

The doctor chewed and grunted. Piper and Shelly waited in dumbstruck silence. The doctor began to moan under his breath. His eyelids fluttered. Finally, Dr. Norris swallowed and cleared his throat. He turned and spoke to Shelly, his voice calm and smooth, his eyes empty and glazed. "We gonna step up on them medicines. You take this new shnitt and come back in time for breakfast tomorrow."

Confusion registered on Shelly's brow. "Breakfast? What?"

"10 A.M. sharp son, we gots to see if them medicines is workin'," the doctor said, leering at Shelly with hungry, glassy eyes.

Dr. Morris Norris scribbled off another prescription and handed it to Shelly. He eyed the sickly youth with curiosity and disdain. He shook his head.

"You dumbass youngs is always gettin' into some bullshnitt," Dr. Norris said. The doctor's words poked hard at Shelly's already fractured self-esteem.

Dr. Norris snorted and pulled a ratty old plastic baggy full of half-smoked cigarettes from his white lab coat pocket. Staring Shelly down, the doctor absent-mindedly reached into the baggy and sifted through the butts. He grabbed one at random, pulled it out, lit it, took an extra-long drag, and promptly exhaled in Shelly's face. "When I was yo age, I had dreams. I wudn't just, forkin' around and, got-damn, gettin' crust 'n shnitt. I had aspirins, I had me some got-damn goals 'n shnitt."

Lost in reverie, Dr. Norris paused and took another long, contemplative drag.

"I tell you I went to school wit Chaz Luger?" Smoke puffed and hissed out of the doctor's mouth and nostrils as he spoke.

Shelly shook his head. He shot a wide, one-eyed glance at Piper. "No, Dr. Norris, you didn't tell us."

"Course I didn't tell you, you little bitch! Why the hell I'd be tellin' you 'bout mah shnitt?!"

Shelly looked perplexed. Piper perked up.

"Actually, doctor, I read about that in my research. You're mentioned in an abbreviated footnote under your stage name, Dr. Nutter. I didn't make the connection until just now. I'm a huge Luger fanatic. To be honest, we both are."

"Well, I'm more of an admirer really," Shelly chimed in with a chuckle.

"Shut the hell up, crusty face," Dr. Norris spat at Shelly. He turned to Piper. "Baby, I like you. You got me feelin' some kinda way. M'm, M'm... damn!"

Piper blushed. Dr. Norris dropped the smoked cigarette on the floor and snuffed it out with his shoe while he rifled through the baggy for another. Finding the one he wanted, he lit the already partially smoked stogie, took a drag, and continued with his story.

"Yeah, that's right baby, Dick Banger's Academy for Aspiring Adult Actors and Anal Assassins..."

Piper and Shelly were enthralled- hanging on the doctor's every word. They couldn't believe it. The honorable Dr. Morris Norris knew Chaz Luger! And Shelly knew that when something is so hard to believe that it becomes appropriate to use the phrase "couldn't believe it," then you knew that, for reals, that shnitt must be true.

"Chaz and me was tight. We'z likes, got-damn, best friends 'n shnitt. He was mah true nilla, know what I'm sayin'. We was both at the top uh the class, bustin' nuts up in bitches day in, day out, Dick Banger the man himself sayin' we'z both the best he ever seen. Then one day this new bitch comes in. She a transfer from the east-side campus. This bitch was for real yo; I ain't never seen nothin' like her befo'. She had a fat ass and she wudn't playin', when she dropped that shnitt, you know that the shnitt was on, know what I'm sayin'? "

Shelly nodded. "Uh-huh..."

Dr. Norris snapped back at Shelly. "Damn son, did I forkin' ask you? Shnitt! Now, as I was sayin'..."

Piper and Shelly leaned in close and listened. The doctor's voice dropped low. This was some serious story time shnitt.

"The faithful day came fo me to do mah scene wit this tight, fine, fat ass ho. My final exam before grad-gee-a-shin. I'z nervous like I ain't never been befo'. It was some real shnitt. The story set up was like, we was on top of a burning building that was underwata in space 'n shnitt and we had to scrump our way to safety. I'z ready to tear that pussy up, but then she gave me them eyes and put that fine-ass booty on me, and it was all over. I could'n holds back... Two pumps an' I'z out..."

Dr. Norris' voice faltered.

"...Chaz had to come in an' finish tha' scene. I failed mah final an' flunked outta school... I lost touch wit Chaz. He gone on an' be a supa-star an' I got tied up in this doctor's game, slingin' medicines 'n shnitt... helpin' dumbass youngs like your crusty ass... and all my dreams dun has been gone... it ain't no way to be livin'..."

The doctor's voice trailed off. He dropped his head, took a final puff of his smoke, and let it drop to the floor. Piper thought she heard him sniffle. Still staring down at the floor, Dr. Norris spoke again, his tone soft with the pain of experience.

"You take them medicines," he said to Shelly without looking up. "That shnitt gonna work."

"If the medicine is going to work, why do I need to come back tomorrow?" Shelly asked.

Shelly's words struck a perturbed nerve in the doctor. He bolted up straight, looking Shelly dead in the eyes.

"Shut the fork up nilla! Go home, take them shnitts, an' come back tomorrow an' bring this fine ass ho' wit 'chu," the doctor blared at Shelly.

"But I...I..." Shelly stammered.

"You best skee-dat, nilla! Get the fork up out my office!"

Piper pulled on Shelly's arm, edging him toward the door. "Come on baby, let's just go."

Shelly turned and let Piper pull him out of the examining room. They walked hurriedly to the front desk. After paying the bill and making another appointment for the next morning, the two dumb ass youngs hopped in Piper's car and drove away.

TEN. Later That Day, Shelly's House

Just as Dr. Norris had prescribed, Shelly took seven of the new pills, stripped out of all his clothes besides his shoes and socks, and stretched out on the couch. Piper nestled a pillow under Shelly's crusty head and covered him up with his favorite blue blanket.

"I feel terrible. Something is really, really, very, very, super-duper wrong, like, for reals," Shelly spoke in a half-conscious drone.

Although she was unsure herself, Piper did her best to comfort her ailing boylyoyly. "Just be still and let the medicine work. It'll be okay, you'll be fine."

Shelly nodded and closed his eyes. Piper sat down in the large brown, puffy chair across the room from him and turned on the TV. She watched the images pass across the screen and her eyes grew heavy. Piper took one last look at Shelly. He was already asleep. *Sleep, how nice,* she thought, just before she closed her eyes and slipped away.

ELEVEN. The Next Morning, Shelly's House

. . . .

Piper was startled awake by the sound of harsh wheezing mixed with crunching and crumbling. She rubbed her eyes and looked over at Shelly. From his head to his shoes, Shelly was encased in the crust, covering every part of him, forming a Shelly-shaped funnel cake boy. Piper blinked and rubbed her eyes again. The funnel cake boy rocked back and forth and jiggled and bounced as if he were trying to roll off the couch.

"Shelly?" Piper said.

She blinked again and looked closer. She saw feet poking out of one end of the crust cocoon.

"Shells!" Piper shouted in alarm, coming fully awake.

Piper fell out of the puffy chair and rolled across the floor to Shelly. She farted twice and sat up next to him. Distorted and frantic words were bubbling up from under the crust. Piper listened in close but couldn't understand the panicked sounds coming from Shelly. She reached up and turned on the Valkos brand Jiffy Translator translating machine that sat on the table next to the couch. She picked up the small microphone that was connected by a curly-q black wire to the small, green metal box covered in knobs and blinking lights. Piper held the microphone out to Shelly and waited. Shelly bounced on the couch, spilling out odd, muffled screeches and sobs that were complimented by the bleeps and bloops of the Jiffy Translator.

The machine whirred and beeped and then printed out a thin slip of paper.

The tiny words read: "Help! Help! I can't breathe!"

While trying not to break down into a total freakout, Piper looked around the room for something to make air holes with. She looked under the couch and pulled out some crochet' needles.

"Yes! Big-ass needles!" She shouted in triumph.

Very carefully Piper made holes for Shelly's nostrils and then a large hole for his mouth. Shelly sucked in huge, frantic gulps of air. Gradually, he stopped writhing and rocking side to side. He settled down and breathed. The couch was covered in crumbs and bits of crust.

"You're all covered up, baby. We need to get you to the honorable doctor Morris Norris right away," Piper said. "I thought you were about to knock yourself off the couch."

"I can't see, Piper, I can't see! You gotta uncover my eyes," Shelly pleaded.

Piper's expression sank. "I don't wanna, baby. It's too risky. Eyeballs are forking tricky, you know. What if I poked those forkers out with these big-ass needles? I wouldn't do it on purpose, but what if I did it anyway? Nobody wants that shnitt, you know."

"Yeah, you're right," Shelly said. "What time is it?"

Piper looked at the wall clock.

"Nine-eighteen, we gotta go." Piper stood up.

"Okay, just help me up," Shelly said.

Piper reached under the mass of crust that covered Shelly's body. Her hands slid between the crust and the couch cushions. Bits of crust tore off and lodged under her fingernails. She felt a light coating of grease smear across her skin, beginning on her hands and spreading up her arms as she slid them further under Shelly's back. She pushed her arms in until her chest was pressed into the crust. Piper took a deep breath and lifted. As she pressed into the crust, the sweet, intoxicating aroma of deep-fried, Gypsy funnel cake goodness seized her mind. Her mouth hung open. A rail of drool dripped from her bottom lip. Her eyes glazed over and turned to slits.

"Fork, you smell good, baby," Piper said in a dazed drawl.

Shelly could hear the intoxication in Piper's voice.

"Please, Piper," He begged, "You have to get me to the doctor right now!"

Piper looked for Shelly's eyes but only saw the greasy, golden crust. "Oh, Shells... I can't see your peepers..."

Sadness welled up inside her.

Piper grunted as she lifted and turned Shelly's body off the couch. His feet touched the floor. Piper breathed in the funnel cake fragrance. She reveled in the smell. Her head swam. She got wet. Heat washed over her body. Her eyelids fluttered and she felt like falling.

Before it was too late, Piper shook her head and came back to the present. Shelly was beginning to tip over. Piper grabbed and steadied him.

Shelly was on his feet. Piper helped him wobble to the car. She propped him up in the front seat and within minutes they were on the road. Within some more minutes, they were parking in front of the office of the honorable Dr. Morris Norris once again. It was five till ten.

"Yes! Take that, tardiness demon! I just made you, my bitch!" Piper shouted.

The small, green tardiness demon that sat cross-legged on the dashboard stood up and stomped his feet. "This isn't over, Piper!"

With a snap of his fingers, the demon twirled and disappeared in a puff of smoke.

"That demon stinks like wet, dirty orphan ass! Get me the fork out of this car!" Shelly hollered.

"He's gone, Shelly!" Piper said. "I've been on time everywhere I've got for the last three months and thirty-three days so he had to leave."

"Good! That forker better not come back. I hated feeling his tiny little eyes on me."

"Tardiness demons are blind, Shelly."

"But they still have eyes! Ugh! Whatever! Just help me out of this stinky forking car!" Shelly squealed, rocking back and forth in his seat.

"Okay, hold on," Piper said, jumping out of the car and hurrying around to Shelly's side.

TWELVE. Ten A.M.

Shelly was spread prone on the examining table, his head area of the crust cocoon propped up on a pile of small pillows. Piper draped a white sheet covered in yellow stains over Shelly to keep him warm. Shelly wondered how many patients, or prostitutes, or both, the doctor had banged on the same stiff padding that he now lay on. He wondered what it had been like to study anal antics alongside Chaz Luger, under the tutelage of Dick Banger, the most legendary producer of adult films of all time. To Shelly, the doctor's life seemed mysterious and full of wonder and things that Shelly could only dream of doing. He imagined what it might be like to live that kind of life. He thought of his own life for a moment and saw it rushing past in a short but beautiful blur, full of colors and feelings and memories. Shelly felt thankful. He hoped there would be more time to make more memories. He hoped this wasn't the end. And Piper sat in the same dingy plastic chair beside him and they waited in silence for the doctor to arrive.

After what felt like minutes, Dr. Norris' theme music began to blast out of the speakers in the ceiling at a deafening volume. Fog poured from vents in the walls, flooding the small room. The overhead lights went down. Lasers bounced off the walls and counters. The door flung open and the honorable Dr. Morris Norris strolled in triumphantly, a short silhouette enshrouded in fog, the hallway bulbs glowing at his back. The door shut by itself behind him. With one hand on his crotch, he lit a full cigarette that dangled from his lips. The music abruptly shut off. The fog stopped rolling in. The laser lights stopped shooting and the harsh fluorescent lights clicked back on.

"What up nillas, let's do this shnitt!" Dr. Norris shouted.

He went to Shelly's side. "You take your medicines?"

Shelly squeaked out a meek "Yes". The crust had become more aggressive and was already threatening to seal Shelly's mouth shut again.

"Then why the hell you still sick?" Dr. Norris asked. "You look like... got-damn... all puffy 'n shnitt."

"I don't know what happened. The medicine didn't work, I guess. I woke up like this," Shelly explained.

"Yeah, he was just... all covered up," Piper added.

"Shnitt... say no mo', say no mo'," said the baffled doctor. He turned to Piper. "Girlyirly, you fine as hell. We 'bout to get turnt up in here."

Piper creased her eyes. "What?" she asked.

Dr. Norris looked back at Shelly. He addressed the room.

"Now, everybody shut the fork up!"

"No one is talking but you," Shelly said.

"I said shut the fork up nilla! Damn!"

The examining room lapsed into complete silence.

"Now, listen good," the doctor whispered.

Piper strained her ears. Dr. Norris quietly puffed on his cigarette. Shelly lay still on the examination table. Piper looked at Shelly. She leaned in closer to him. Her eyes went wide when she heard it: the faint sound of deep-frying dough.

"This can't be possible," she whispered to the doctor.

"Oh, but it is." Dr. Norris whispered back. "Smell it, bitch."

The sweet aroma of the highly addictive, psychoactive, deep-fried gypsy funnel cake flooded Piper's senses. She inhaled deep and long. She drooled. Her stomach ached and rumbled and her eyes rolled back in her head. A wave of heat blew over her as if from some invisible deep fryer. She licked her lips and moaned.

A sudden twinge of guilt hit Piper and brought her back from her revelry. She slapped herself on both cheeks and rubbed her eyes.

"Oh, my shnitt, oh fork, he's frying on the inside! I can hear it! I can smell it!" Piper cried. Her breasts bounced with panic. "Do something, doctor! Help him!"

Shelly squeaked. The crust had once again grown over most of his mouth.

"—Elp... meee!" Shelly squeaked out through the crust.

"Ah-ight, I'm gone do somethin'," the doctor said.

Piper looked frantic. "Hurry, the crust is covering him up again! It's all in his mouth hole and it's covering his nose holes back up too!"

Dr. Norris' eyes were bloodshot and red. His expression took on a grave appeal. "Girlyirly,

this ain't no normal crust. This is some gypsy shnitt. He turnin' into a got-damn funnel cake. Now ain't that some shnitt!"

"It is... it's some shnitt, for reals!" Piper said, on the verge of laughing.

She felt her eyes growing heavy again. The aroma of gypsy funnel cake enticed her taste buds. A gnawing hunger grew inside her. Her clit twitched. Her feet felt like puffy clouds.

The doctor stared into her glassy eyes; his face had gone blank. His mouth hung open.

"I'm gone do somethin'," he mumbled as he wavered back and forth in a slight, stutter-step motion.

The air of the small examining room was thick with the fragrance of frying dough, heavy oil, syrup, and sugar.

"Pease... elp... meee...!" Shelly cried out, his puffy, crusty body bumping up and down on the table.

Piper breathed in deep and swooned, falling into the doctor and nearly knocking him over. He caught her and they crumbled into giggles.

Dr. Norris pointed at Shelly. "He sound like a 'lil bitch," the doctor said as he doubled over and howled with laughter.

"Elp meee!" Piper squealed in a high-pitched imitation of Shelly, her words barely slipping out between the laughs that threatened to choke her.

"Got-damn he smell so good though!" The doctor exclaimed, his eyes puffy, glazed, and hanging half-closed.

Piper drooled on herself. "I'm so... so... so forkin' horny, I mean, hungry... hungry. I wanna eat... I wanna eat and..." Piper's voice dropped off low. "...I wanna foorrkk..."

"Go on girlyirly, take you a bite," Dr. Norris said, looking and pointing down at Shelly.

Shelly's feet twitched. Dough was rising out of his shoes where his feet were going through the metamorphosis. The sound of frying grew louder.

"Waat's appening?" Shelly called out from underneath the crust.

Dr. Norris leaned down close to Shelly. "You's forkin' blind, bitch!" He shouted, laughing, poking the golden puffs over Shelly's eyes with his middle finger. "You don' know what tha fork is goin' on!"

Piper and the doctor filled the room to overflowing with laughter. Stumbling and clutching at one another, they fell onto Shelly. The crust-covered boy bounced on the table and began to shake.

Dr. Norris and Piper stopped laughing and backed away from the table as Shelly's body spasmed in a violent fit. He screeched and screamed from inside his funnel cake casing. The sounds of bubbling grease and frying dough grew louder and louder until they reached a fevered pitch.

Then, the sounds abruptly stopped.

Piper laughed out loud in amazement as the room fell silent once again. She heard Shelly crying underneath the doughy crust and unexpected sorrow filled her heart.

"Oh Shelly, baby, I'm so sorry for laughing at you. I don't know what's happening. I don't understand. I'm so sorry."

Piper bent over and kissed Shelly where she thought his forehead would be. She moved her lips over his doughy, golden face to where his eyes should be. Sniffling floated up from deep within the crust. Thick, brown liquid burped to the surface and oozed down Shelly's face.

Piper smelled Maple syrup. Her eyes grew heavy again. Her magic lady parts tingled with wanting.

She bent down and kissed Shelly lightly where his lips would have been. Her lips tingled. She kissed him again, opening her mouth wide and caressing Shelly's golden crust with her tongue.

Grease spread across Piper's lips. Heat and wetness bloomed between her legs. She kissed Shelly yet again, letting her lips linger. She pressed in hard and moaned. She moved her tongue over the doughy, crusty surface. She opened her mouth wider, pushed down as hard as she could, and bit into the funnel cake boy. An agonized scream reverberated through the room as Piper bit off Shelly's lips.

Streams of thick, brown liquid poured out from where Shelly's eyes used to be. Bright red bubbled up from where his lips had been. Piper licked at the liquid while she chewed.

"His tears are made of maple syrup. His blood tastes like strawberry," Piper said, her voice languid and dreamy.

Piper took another bite. She rubbed herself through the thin fabric of her lime green skirt.

The doctor moved in behind her. Piper felt his hard thickness in the crease of her ass. She felt his breath hot on her cheek. He was bent over her.

"Bitch, gimme some of that shnitt," he said.

"Which shnitt are you talking about, doctor?" Piper asked, looking back over her shoulder with an impish grin.

Dr. Norris ran his hands over her breasts and her thighs and all her lovely places. "All the shnitt," he panted into Piper's ear hole.

And Shelly cried. And then he screamed. "I'm 'til a-wive! I'm 'til a-wive! P-wease, don' eat me!"

Piper looked at Shelly through red, glazed, slits. "I'm sorry baby," she said. "I don't mean to eat you, but I can't stop. You're just so forking delicious."

She ripped off Shelly's ear and handed it to Dr. Norris. Shelly squealed and cried, his once high voice crackling as his vocal cords slowly turned into fried dough.

"Mmmmmm... damn that is some good shnitt!" The doctor said, rubbing his crotch on Piper who leaned further over Shelly.

Piper dug her fingers deep into Shelly's crispy, doughy face and pulled. A doughnut-sized chunk of dough flesh tore away in her grip. Red strawberry blood spewed up out of Shelly's torn face. Piper held her mouth over the tiny fountain and slurped up the thick liquid. The blood spurted and splattered into her mouth and onto her lips and her face. She rose and gasped for air. The doctor licked the blood off Piper's cheek.

"Shnitt girlyirly, you ain' lyin', he blood do taste like strawberry!" Dr. Norris proclaimed.

Piper rubbed the dough all over her face, soaking up the strawberry blood before cramming it all into her mouth. Closing her eyes, she chewed and moaned and basked in the pleasure of the tasty sensation. Still chewing, she turned around and faced Dr. Norris. Piper tore more crusty fried dough off Shelly and fed it to the doctor in a languid motion. She looked at his groin and saw his desire for her bulging in his pants, threatening to jump out and eat her alive.

Shelly's crying faded into the distance as Piper's eyes melded into Dr. Morris Norris' gaze. She pointed at the bulge in his pants.

"What are you gonna do with that?" She asked coyly.

Piper's words danced a sultry trip. Blood, death, and honey dripped from every curvy syllable. The doctor's response came low and deep.

"Bitch, I think you know what I'm 'bout to gonna do... what 'chu gonna do?"

With her eyes locked on Dr. Norris, Piper ripped another piece of crusty flesh off of Shelly.

A dough-muffled scream came from the helpless boylyoyly. "Top eaing meeee!! I'm 'til a-wive!!"

Piper broke the flesh bread in half and fed the doctor. "Flesh of my flesh, blood of my blood," she said, giggling blasphemously.

Piper turned back around, bent over Shelly, and started biting into his face. Dr. Norris pressed up against her. He tugged at her skirt and her panties until they slid down her legs to the floor. Piper stepped out of her clothes and kicked them away. The doctor stepped back and stripped down to his white socks, which he pulled up to his knees. Stark nude, he did three push-ups and then put his off-white lab coat back on.

The honorable doctor honed his scalpel and cut off Piper's shirt and bra and she never even looked up. She just kept eating. And Shelly kept crying.

Dr. Norris slid his massive meat member up and down Piper's crack. "I was the wonder of da Academy. I was havin' the smallest dick at that damn school, but I made miracles wit what I had. Mir-culls, bitch!"

The doctor reached over Piper and tore another chunk of Shelly's face off. He dug his fingers in deep, soaking them in strawberry syrup blood.

Dr. Norris shoved the dough into his mouth. He reached down and slathered the blood syrup over Piper's sweet love muffin. Dipping his first two fingers in Shelly's blood, the doctor spit on his fingers and slid them deep inside Piper. He slathered his fingers with more blood and rubbed it inside her and outside her.

Piper groaned in ecstasy while she crunched down on Shelly's crusty doughy flesh. She was hot. She was soaked and dripping. Dr. Norris took his fingers out of Piper and licked them clean.

"Damn girlyirly, you taste like moldy strawberries. M'm... M'm!"

Piper laughed and then let out a loud gasp as Dr. Morris Norris drove his man sausage into her hot lady box. He went in deep, deeper than she'd ever felt before, and she loved it.

I can't believe it, Piper thought. *I'm getting nailed by Chaz Luger's ex-best friend. This is like some sixth degree of separation shnitt, like, for real.*

And Piper smiled a smile like none she'd ever smiled before as she tore a massive hole in her helpless boylyboy's chest. And Dr. Norris forked her like she'd never been forked before.

Blind behind his useless, encrusted eyes, Shelly felt every movement of their bodies as Dr. Norris made hot, sweet, sticky, passionate, slimy love to Piper, *his girlyirly, his Piper,* right there on top of him, where Shelly heard every sigh and every erotic moan, and they didn't even fucking care.

Shelly felt Piper's teeth in his new doughy flesh. He heard his voice whimpering in his head. He felt all of his organs morphing into dough and fruit compote. And above every sound and sensation, above all the pain of transformation, were his lover and the doctor going at it, pushing and moaning on top of him.

Piper would be cumming soon. Shelly could hear it in her voice. His thoughts wandered to memories of being inside her- of having her in a chair, or on a table, or up against a wall. She would scream so loud. She would say that she liked it. She would say that she liked *him*.

The memories warmed him.

They mixed with the voices floating over him and he felt his cock grow and thicken and get hard. Shelly got harder and harder even though he didn't want to, he couldn't help it. His doughy dick turned stale and brittle from the erection.

Piper's weight shifted. Her body fell hard onto the section over Shelly's crusty hard cock, causing his dick to shatter into a billion crumbs. A sea of silent maple syrup tears flooded out of the creases where Shelly's eyeballs used to be. His screams of pain and humiliation and betrayal remained nestled in his mind because his mouth was gone and his throat had turned to dough. He was still cooking on the inside.

His breath was evaporating.

His feet twitched.

He felt his flesh being torn away and yet his mind went on. He felt the bodies and mouths press down on him and of all the thoughts that came and went in a seemingly endless blur, one thought persisted, one thought remained, and one thought tormented him: *I'm still alive. I'm still alive. I'm. Still. Alive.*

• • • •

PIPER'S NAILS DUG DEEPER into Shelly's fried dough flesh. Strawberry syrup blood oozed and pooled around her fingertips. Her breasts bounced as Dr. Norris pounded into her again and again and again. She was revving up. Her climax was building. She was going to scream. She curled both of her hands and tore off handfuls of funnel cake flesh. Strawberry syrup blood covered her hands and dripped from her fingers. She shoved one fistful into her mouth. Without hesitating she crammed the second fistful in behind the first.

With her mouth packed full, Piper chewed and moaned. She smeared strawberry syrup blood on her breasts. She was moaning and chewing with her mouth open and rubbing her breasts with one hand while digging into Shelly's ravaged dessert flesh with the other. Bits of half-chewed cake mixed with drool and saliva rolled out of Piper's mouth and clung to her chin and hung there like stranded dingleberries. She chewed on the huge wad of dough flesh in her mouth.

She started to cum.

She started to scream.

"Oh... Oh... Fork me Ch—!" Piper began.

As the words to her favorite line to scream during orgasm began to roar out of her ("Fork me, Chaz Luger!!"), Dr. Norris thrust into her especially hard and knocked her off balance.

Just as Piper was screaming and swallowing at the same time, her steadying hand slipped off what was left of Shelly's chest. Her words and the wad of masticated funnel cake flesh lodged in her throat as she slammed face down into the pool of strawberry syrup blood that had collected in the small crater in Shelly's chest.

Dr. Norris pounded into her, sending her face deeper into the goo. Piper's grease and syrup-covered hands slipped on the sides of the examining table as she struggled to push herself up. Dr. Norris' strong hand on her back held her down. Piper's arms flailed.

Enraptured in this moment of magic and bliss, the doctor's eyes were squeezed shut. "I'm 'bout to bust a nut up in this bitch!" he proclaimed. "Yay-Yuh!"

Piper convulsed under the weight of the former would-be anal assassin superstar. As Dr. Norris jack-hammered away on Piper's skinny frame, he began his trademark "countdown to nuttin' call-outs."

"Bitch! Bitch! Rims! Club! Muh-nay!" He called out, with a word for every thrust. "Rims! Muh-nay! Rims! Muh-nay! Club!"

The doctor was closer now. He was almost there. As his climax rose inside him, all the shapes, colors, and hard lines in the examining room blurred into squiggly lines and shifting waves of color. Dr. Norris faded into the blur, becoming a squirming mass of orange and white, until the lines and colors reassembled. He looked around. It was a gypsy funnel cake-induced hallucination! He was back in his old classroom at the academy.

• • • •

THAT DAY'S LESSON WAS on rhythm and thrusting technique. The movie set that was built in the classroom was made up to be the main deck of the ship of a time-traveling Renaissance fair-themed puppet show that had gotten stranded in the year 3035 after their space machine had run out of Valkos brand pubic hair removal lotion, which had turned out to be a key component of the time travel formula.

The mood aboard the *SS Frolic* was grim as the troupe had been en route to the Intergalactic Time Travelling Puppeteers Award Show and Banquette, where they were to be awarded the best adult puppet show. However, sadly, their ship had broken down.

The crew was disheartened, but, as Captain McSpooge, portrayed with emotional conviction by Dr. Nutter, was demonstrating, the obvious way to fix the spaceship and get to the award ceremony on time was to have loads of crazy sex.

On set as Captain McSpooge that day, Morris Norris was putting his all into the lesson. He was in his happy place. He knew he was doing what Allah had made him to do.

Morris's instructor sat behind the camera, looking on, scribbling occasional notes on a pad of paper attached to a clipboard. His classmates watched with pure admiration. Morris looked over to his best pal Chaz, who sat nearby watching him work. Chaz smiled wide and gave Morris the thumbs up.

The woman who was bent over in front of Morris howled with pleasure. He held her hips in his small, pudgy hands, thrusting into her from behind, his frilly costume shirt bouncing with each movement. He looked over his admiring classmates and smiled wide because he knew he was the best they'd ever seen. His cock worked miracles- he was a Giddydamn hero.

• • • •

DR. NORRIS BLINKED and he was back in the stale and dirty examining room. He looked down on Piper's pale skin and grinned.

"I don't need no camera or no classroom to do tha Lord's work!" He shouted. "Here it comes!"

The honorable Dr. Morris Norris slammed into Piper so hard that her feet left the floor. He went into a frenzy of erratic thrusts and gyrations.

"Bitch, bitch, bitch... Chaamm——Paaggnneeee!!!!" Dr. Norris screamed as he erupted. For a moment he couldn't feel his body. He seemed to be floating in the ether. Time was suspended. He hovered in an orgasmic billow of sugar and grease.

And while the doctor pounded and shoved and hollered and came, Piper choked and gasped and clutched at the frayed hope that she wasn't, truly, for real, like, totally about to die.

Piper's fears and worries over her own possibly imminent demise mixed with a sudden surging orgasm that wracked her being and caused collisions of time and space. In an unexpected instant, Piper was cumming and cumming and cumming harder than she'd ever cum before. She wanted to scream but she had no breath left for screaming. She slapped her palms on the sides of the examining table. Her face turned a dark blue. Thin, choking gasps fell from her lips. Her eyelids flittered and snapped shut.

• • • •

AND THEN, IN A FLITTERING instant, Piper was in a lush, tree-lined field. It was the end of a warm summer's day. The evening sun bathed the field in a deep orange and purple glow. Piper wore her favorite green short shorts and a trusty yellow tank top. Soft grass caressed her bare feet. Shelly stood next to her wearing nothing but a white bow tie and his pink man thong that Piper had given him for their six-day anniversary. He held out his hand and smiled. She put her hand in his and felt its warmth.

"Where are they?" Piper asked as she turned and looked around the field.

"They'll be here soon," Shelly replied.

"Are you sure?"

"Shnitt yeah, they're always on time," Shelly said, grinning wide.

A swooshing sound surrounded them and a great wind swept through the field. Piper brushed her scraggly, greasy hair out of her eyes and looked around. A thousand Ninja women stood in the field, creating a perfect circle around the young couple.

"Did they come from heaven?" Piper asked.

Shelly nodded. "Shnitt yeah, they did."

"Am I going to heaven, Shells?"

Shelly ran his finger along Piper's cheek and up to her hair, brushing back the greasy, electric blue mess. "There's nowhere else to go."

Piper smiled at Shelly and saw his beautiful and vulnerable soul in his eyes. The Ninja women took recorders and kazoos out of their shirt pockets and pressed them to their lips.

Allah's voice boomed down from the clouds, counting them in, "And a one, a two, a one, two, three, four!"

Piper recognized the music from the very first note as the Ninja women eased into

"Blondie's Theme", the highlight from the original score of *Friday Night Fuckfest in F Minor*, and Piper's all-time favorite song.

The kazoos and recorders rang out into the fading light of the evening. Shelly took both of Piper's hands in his and looked deep into her eyes.

"Will you dance with me?" He asked.

"Yes," Piper said with a deep smile, nodding her head.

Shelly pulled Piper close and took her in his arms. She rested her head on his chest and together they swayed to the soft, smooth jazz sounds. A gentle breeze passed over them.

"Shell..." Piper whispered.

"Yes, Piper..."

"I'm sorry I ate you."

Shelly chuckled lightly, which made Piper do the same.

"That's okay, Piper. And I'm sorry that I was such a whiney twit. I should've appreciated you more. You were my best friend."

"Don't worry, Shell, all that shnitt is over now." She squeezed him tightly to her. They stopped swaying.

"Am I still your best friend?" Piper asked.

"Yes, Piper, you always will be."

Shelly wrapped his arms tight around Piper. He pressed his cheek against her forehead and they held each other close.

"You too," Piper said softly as a tear fell from her eye.

Shelly kissed Piper on the top of her head and the Ninjas went into the last stanza of the song. Piper raised her head and looked up at Shelly. He leaned down and kissed her eyes, gathering her tears on his lips. Piper closed her eyes. She felt Shelly's lips light upon her own and tasted the salt of her tears. Her hands felt the skin rise on his bare back. He put his hand on her cheek. Piper opened her eyes.

"Is it time to go?" She asked.

Shelly nodded and smiled.

The music surrounding them grew louder and Shelly and Piper turned and looked out into the field. A loud crack sounded from above and a pink bubble gum staircase descended from the clouds. Piper and

Shelly smiled at each other and, hand in hand, they walked toward the stairs. The Ninja women wound back into the opening bars of "Blondie's Theme" as they filed in behind Shelly and Piper, following them up the stairs. Shelly squeezed Piper's hand.

"I like you, Piper," he said.

"I like you too, Shelly," Piper replied.

And they laughed and smiled as they ascended into the clouds, followed by a thousand Ninja women playing Piper's favorite song.

• • • •

IN THE DINGEY DOCTOR'S examining room, a slight grin broke out across Piper's blue lips as she took her last breath. And then there was no breath at all.

Piper collapsed and her body was still. Dr. Norris gave three more pumps and fell on top of her, his cock still hard inside Piper's very recently deceased and still warm corpse.

Shelly listened. He heard the doctor's heaving breaths as they grew faint and dim. His heart turned into a pile of blueberry compote and stopped beating forever.

THIRTEEN. Twenty Seconds Later

A timer on the sink counter sounded its harsh alarm. Dr. Norris sprang up and pulled out of Piper.

He slapped Piper's ass. "Shnitt, baby, that was some good shnitt! Now I'm ready for a snack! You hungry?"

Dr. Norris nudged Piper. She didn't move, or speak, or breathe. He bent down and put his ear on her bare back. He listened. No heartbeat.

"Damn!" Dr. Norris whispered in alarm. "Fine ass bitch done got forked to death!"

He felt a swell of pride. "I done kilt that damn thot wit mah dick!" The doctor smiled. "I'm a got-damn hero!"

Dr. Norris raised his head high, pulled Piper's corpse off Shelly's half-eaten body, and dropped her in the corner. While he was smoking a post-nut cigarette and wondering when the incinerator would be available so he could dispose of Piper's remains, the irresistible aroma of deep-fried funnel cake drifted into his nostrils. His eyes glazed over. Saliva filled his mouth. With his still semi-hard rod dangling in the breeze, the doctor stumbled to the dead funnel cake boy. His hands were eager and his eyes were huge with lust. He tossed his unfinished cigarette across the room.

Dr. Norris hunched over. He plunged his hands into the hole in Shelly's chest, pulled from side to side, and ripped it wide open. A tide of strawberry syrup blood flowed out onto the examining table and began to drip on the floor.

Shelly's entrails were easy to remove. They were crispy on the outside and soft on the inside.

The doctor tore into them with a ravenous hunger. He felt insatiable. Shelly's intestines tasted so good that the doctor got hard again.

Dr. Norris lubed up his man meat with strawberry blood and maple syrup tears. He stroked his cock with one hand and tore off pieces of cake and shoveled them into his mouth with the other. He jerked his dick harder and faster as he ate in a lunatic binge. Then the jerking off and eating piece by piece wasn't enough.

He had to have more.

He had to have it all.

Overwhelmed, Dr. Norris plunged his dick deep inside Shelly's soft, dead-dough body. He sank his teeth into Shelly's funnel cake face. He gnawed the soft sweet flesh and called out garbled phrases of pure delight. He ripped and tore and pounded the delectable dessert corpse. His scalp tingled. His cock throbbed. The sugar and grease coursed through his veins. Dr. Norris felt it rising inside him- He was going to erupt.

He wanted to watch.

He wanted to see his beautiful jizz.

He wanted to paint the walls with his cum.

The doctor pulled out. He sat up on his knees, hunching over Shelly's mutilated carcass on the small examining table, furiously hammering his cock while he ate.

And the more the doctor ate, the harder the doctor stroked, until finally, hollering with his mouth full, he erupted.

The doctor couldn't believe his eyes, for it truly was a sight to see.

A solid stream of thick, pure, hot golden grease shot out of his knob nozzle and sprayed all over Shelly's remains. The doughy flesh sizzled and fried as the doctor's searing grease load splashed over the soft surface.

"Bitch, bitch, bitch! This here mu-forka gone be, got-damn, exra crispy now!" Dr. Norris exclaimed, his lips quivering in anticipation.

The doctor worked his hose from side to side, spraying the scalding grease all over Shelly's corpse. Shelly's pastry skin popped and sizzled. Steam rose from its extra crispy surface.

Dr. Norris jerked his meat stick harder and harder. His face was wild with mania. The stream of grease dwindled to spurts until there was nothing. But the doctor felt something else inside.

His mind wandered back to his twenty-third birthday when he had boned a legless, blind, paraplegic, excommunicated Baptist secretary in a dumpster behind the optometrist's office. He smiled and hammered his dick faster and faster. He was going to bust another one. He was almost there. He felt the explosion rising.

"Bitch,   bitch,   bitch!   Rims!   Club!   Muh-Nay! Chaamm——Paaggnneeee!!" Dr. Norris screamed.

He thrust his hips upward as a massive, blinding puff of pure white powdered sugar cum shot out of his cock.

The doctor screeched with delight as he shot out another puff, then another, and still another, aiming and firing and covering the funnel cake boy in saccharine sweet yummy goodness.

Torrents of drool flowed out over Dr. Norris's lips and down his chin. He blew his last load of powdered sugar jizz, leaned back on his knees, and appreciated his work.

"I'ms a got-damn hero," he said to himself. "If only Chaz wuh here to see it..."

"I'm always here," said a voice from behind the doctor- a voice that dripped honey and cried gold, a voice that Morris Norris knew better than any other voice in the whole wide Giddydamn world.

The doctor's head snapped to the side.

Chaz Luger stood in the corner, looming tall over Piper's dead body, naked except for his very own patented brand of Chaz Luger's Fork and Run running shoes, stroking his award-winning cock.

"Chaz! It you!" The doctor shouted.

"Yep, it sure is," Chaz replied in his velvety smooth tone. He winked and flashed his brilliantly white smile.

"You seen what I done, Chaz? You seen?" Dr. Norris asked.

"I saw it," Chaz replied. "I'm always watching, buddy. I'm so proud of you for what you've accomplished here today. This work that you're doing, these miracles that you're making, it's much, much more important than anything I've ever done. I may have the fame and notoriety and millions of dollars but you, you, my dear friend and brother of the cock, you have the vision."

Tears filled Morris's eyes and spilled down his cheeks. His chest heaved as sobs wracked his body.

"Why'd you leave me, Chaz? We wuz tight, you an' me, like, bes' friends 'n shnitt."

Chaz shifted his weight and raised his left eyebrow. His cock stroking took on a more thoughtful demeanor as he carefully considered his next words. He cleared his throat and looked at Morris with his trademark expression of utmost earnestness.

"I didn't leave you, buddy, you pushed me away. After you failed your final exam, you pushed us all away because you thought you weren't good enough. And, of course, that wasn't true at all. It wasn't then and it's not now- you're the best, and you always will be. You're a Giddydamn hero."

Tears of joy blurred Morris's vision. He couldn't speak. He stared at Chaz with adoring eyes.

"Well, I gotta boogie," Chaz said.

He closed his eyes in concentration, jerking his dick harder and faster. Angel's wings sprouted out of his back. He opened his eyes, smiled at Morris, and spread his wings wide.

"Just remember what I said, buddy, and let go of the past. That stuff doesn't mean anything anymore." He angled his superhuman dick down on Piper's body. "You're the best!"

Chaz started moaning. "Here I go!" He shouted. "3... 2... 1... Blast off!"

Chaz called out in rapture as a stream of fire blasted out of his mammoth penis, engulfing Piper's body in flames, and blasting him into the air.

His wings flapped as he burst through the ceiling, the roof, and into the sky above, shouting out, "You're free! Free to laugh, free to live... free to fuck!"

"Why is you misquotin' you most famous lines?" Morris shouted at Chaz, who was now high above the building.

"It's a special moment, buddy, don't ruin it with pointless questions!" Chaz shouted, his voice trailing down from the clouds.

Morris laughed to himself. He watched Chaz fly further and further away until he was just a speck. And then he was gone.

"Thank you, Chaz, thank you," Morris whispered under his breath. One last tear drop fell from his eye. He stood staring at the empty hole in the ceiling when the aroma of fried dough floated up to him again.

Dr. Norris looked down at Shelly and then back up at the ceiling. All the moldy, green, and black spotted tiles were back in their usual place. He looked at Piper. Her pale corpse was slumped in the corner without a burn mark in sight.

The doctor's mouth hung open.

"I had me a got-damn vision!" He shouted. "Ya-Yuh!"

He bent over what was left of Shelly and inhaled deep. He felt his hands in the sugar and on the hot, greasy, crispy, crusty dough as he pressed down on the funnel cake boy.

"I'm gone make a mir-cull for you, Chaz! A got-damn mir-cull!" He hollered into the empty room.

Then he ate like he'd never eaten before.

· · · ·

THE DOCTOR RIPPED INTO Shelly's corpse.

Screaming and cursing, he punched and tore at Shelly's head, ripping chunks of the fried dough flesh off until the young man's head was gone. Then onward into Shelly's neck, the doctor went, working his way down. He hunched over and slurped strawberry syrup blood out of Shelly's neck stump. He dug in with his teeth, inhaling the golden delight until Shelly's neck was gone. A flood of sticky red poured out of the trashed cadaver.

Then, most of Shelly's left shoulder was gone. Heat flooded over the doctor's body. He slapped his protruding belly and whooped and hollered. He was pouring sweat but still he ate.

The doctor thrust his pelvis and clawed at Shelly's chest and torso, ripping his way across to the right shoulder. Most of Shelly's right shoulder was going too. The doctor felt his own body expanding.

He squealed with delight. "Oh, you so forkin' good, son! You so forkin' good!"

His cheeks bulged. His face was swathed in powdered sugar cum and strawberry syrup blood. Dr. Norris breathed harder and harder. A sharp pain ripped through his tender stomach. At that point, he wanted to stop eating but his steam shovel hands wouldn't stop moving. They kept filling his mouth with the twice-fried dessert. His gums kept flapping. His teeth kept chewing. His throat kept swallowing.

His skin swelled and stretched. Fear mingled with pleasure in his mind. Maple syrup tears began to fall from his eyes. Sweat trickled down his forehead and onto his lips. He ran his tongue over his lips and a salty sweet buttery flavor filled his mouth. He looked at his arms. Butter sweat gushed out of every pore. Dr. Norris licked his arm.

"Oh shnitt," he muttered in astonishment. "I'm forkin' delicious!"

The doctor's stomach twisted into knots. His creamy orange skin started to turn yellow. And heat burned through him, getting hotter and hotter with every passing moment. Morris Norris squeezed his eyes shut and panted.

Dr. Norris reached out to pull another chunk of flesh off Shelly's torso. He couldn't feel his left hand. He opened his eyes and looked down.

His left hand was gone. In its place was a dripping stump, melted at the wrist. Disgusted with himself, the doctor licked at his stump. He tasted butter sweat, raspberry blood, and grease. He licked at his melting arm, slurping up every drop. He reached out with his right hand to tear off a hunk of dough and smear it across his stump.

Dr. Norris no longer had a right hand. He leaned over to try and rub his right stump over Shelly's remains.

"I gots to try me a bite wit this got-damn ras-berry 'n butta," he said.

The doctor moved slowly, holding his dripping, melting stumps over what was left of Shelly. Leaning in, he lost his balance and fell face down into the funnel cake corpse. For a second Dr. Norris struggled to breathe until he realized he'd rather eat than breathe.

He ate his way deep inside of Shelly, to a place where there was no reason to breathe or live or want to do either of those things. The doctor's face melted off and joined with the goo inside Shelly's soul case. He licked at himself until his tongue was gone. He slurped up his buttery greasy body until his mouth became a useless puddle of raspberry butter.

And as the honorable Dr. Morris Norris dissolved into a pool of human syrup and grease, he couldn't help but think, *got-damn, I'm fuckin' delicious!*

The End

Friday Night Fuckfest in F Minor: A Critical Analysis

By

Harry Cox

75

Friday Night Fuckfest in F Minor (2007) is the sixty-ninth film by acclaimed erotica writer, rock musician, and adult filmmaker Mandy De Sandra. Now considered Ms. De Sandra's finest work, the film is also heralded as a modern classic that transcends all genres as well as perceived socio-economic divides. Although *Friday Night Fuckfest in F Minor* appears on the surface to be a hyper-sexualized romp that parodies its passions, upon closer inspection it reveals itself as a film that celebrates the rejection of so-called physical handicaps, abnormalities, or limitations, and champions personal sexual empowerment and freedom while calling for a deeper, more spiritually enlightened approach to one's sexuality.

The film opens with the protagonist, a sweaty and inebriated "Blondie" Phelps Martini, on stage in a dingy, smoke-filled nightclub, wailing away on a saxophone with a smooth jazz quartet. Blondie, played by the legendary Chaz Luger in his debut, break-out role, is filled with passion. He thrusts his hips as he plays, his exquisite fingers massaging the saxophone keys, his sensuous lips curled tight around the horn's mouthpiece, his body language implying that he is making love to the audience through his music, which itself acts as an extension of his penis, his love, his sex drive. Indeed, the audience responds by offering orgasmic sighs and lustful ogling of the heated jazz musician commanding the stage. It should be noted here that in all of the film's live music scenes, the music was actually performed by the actors themselves and recorded live on set at the insistence of Mandy De Sandra, who was striving to give the film a raw, gritty, documentary feel and atmosphere, the effect of which was spectacularly achieved by improvised lines, scenes, and live music.

After the band finishes their set, Blondie is approached by a star-struck tuba player from an Eastern European, touring orchestra. Through a series of brief dialog exchanges, the attractive stranger successfully woos Blondie, and he leads her to the backstage area. Using voyeuristic cinematography techniques, we witness all the antics as if we were a fly floating in the backstage ether as Blondie and the mystery woman tackle every known position on every conceivable surface in what is arguably one of the most intensely passionate scenes of pure sexual prowess ever captured on film. Staying true to the director's ideals and aesthetics, the twenty-six-minute scene is filmed documentary style, with one camera and no cuts. It is through this unadorned style that the raw beauty and energy of the uninhibited sexual experience are transmitted with no filter to the viewing audience.

Following their final, shared orgasm, Blondie and the woman collapse onto the dirty backstage couch where they fall into a deep sleep. With breath-taking visual effect trickery, Mandy De Sandra leads us through a distorted dream in which Blondie revisits each step in his rise to the middle of the Mable Town smooth jazz scene, where success meets inevitable excess and we see Phelps recalling visions of drinks, drugs, and women, each image becoming successively blurrier and more distorted than the last. Veteran composer Dick Mayhem's score takes a dark turn as the dreamy images become more and more nightmarish until, at a horrific atonal crescendo, Blondie is jarred awake. He looks around the filthy little room, naked and alone, his head throbbing, his stomach turning, surrounded by empty bottles and small baggies filled with white powdery residue. His facial expression begs, "What have I done and why have I done it again?" He rubs his eyes and realizes that his fingers feel different. He blinks. The camera pulls focus, and, from Blondie's perspective, we see that his fingers have turned into penises. A scream roars from his throat and fills the small room. With a solitary Blondie in tears, fearing that he will never play his beloved saxophone again, the still shot fades to black.

The next shot is of Blondie in a doctor's examining room, receiving the news that he has contracted an incurable sexually transmitted disease that has turned his fingers into penises. The starkly lit room coupled with the lonely piano accompaniment gives the scene a somber feeling of hopelessness and loss. Eschewing the well-worn formula of a doctor, nurse, and patient three-way scene, De Sandra instead chooses to capitalize on the feelings of loneliness, isolation, and dread that Blondie is experiencing. After leaving the doctor's office, a montage set to Dick Mayhem's masterful, heart-wrenching minor key r & b lament, "What the Fuck is I Supposed to do (Now That I've Got Dicks for Fingers?)" fully illustrates our hero's descent into complete despair, taking the audience into the grimiest back alleys and roach motels, where Blondie spends his days and nights wearing oven mitts on his hands and guzzling cheap gin and mouthwash. One morning while Phelps is relieving himself of cheap gin behind a dumpster in the alley, a saxophone plummets from a nearby apartment window, striking the destitute musician on his back. After spraying urine on himself, he turns to see the instrument lying in front of him on a small pile of trash, glistening in the early morning sun like a vision from heaven. Tears fill Blondie's eyes as he throws off the oven mitts and picks up the sax. Cautiously, Phelps puts his lips to the mouthpiece and his penis fingers on the keys. The camera closes in on his eyes and the deep lines of fear and concentration that cover his forehead. There is a silent pause and then... he plays. The sonorous glory echoes through the alley as Blondie jams his heart out. To his wonder and surprise, not only can he play with penis fingers, but he sounds smoother and jazzier, and better than ever before. It is here that we get a glimpse of De Sandra's philosophy that so-called "disabilities" or "abnormalities" can prove to be an invaluable asset that improves the individual, and, therefore, instead of attempting to rid ourselves of such "imperfections" we should embrace and capitalize on them.

Following his revelation in the alley, "Blondie" Phelps Martini is reunited with his band, playing to sell-out audiences, and pleasing hordes of insatiable groupies. At the end of a whirlwind year of success after success, Blondie is awarded the Smoothest Smooth Jazzer in the Universe award, an award which comes with a recording contract with

Smooth Move Records, a one-trillion dollar signing bonus, and ultimate fame and glory. Truly he had arrived as he moved into a palace and bought a saxophone made of pure gold. But, as is usually the case, the fame, glory, and excess of luxury prove to be too much for young Blondie as he descends into a dark and life-threatening cough syrup addiction, which sends him swirling into a deep depression. During a particularly massive cough syrup binge, De Sandra employs psychedelic camera work to illustrate Phelps' state of mind, bending colors and using an array of wide lenses and "man-cam" POV shots to bring the audience into our protagonist's headspace as Blondie makes love to ghosts, screams at walls, and tries to climb inside a bathtub faucet. At the height of his hysteria, Phelps runs naked from his palace, screaming into the night, where he is captured in the streets by the ruthless East Mable Town mob boss, Princess Lai Me Coochie Dawg, whose henchwomen knock Blondie out and take him to their underground lair.

When Blondie awakens the next day, he is taken in front of the Princess where he is informed that he must perform private smooth jazz gigs and sexy antics for the Princess and her harem if he wishes to stay alive.

Another montage follows with Phelps pleasing the women of the harem with his music and his body, a groundbreaking editing technique introduced by De Sandra as a way to pack a lot of sexiness into a short amount of time, and one that would be often imitated but never executed as successfully as it is here. It is in this movement of the film that we see Blondie forced into a life of excess. He is regularly bathed, his body is rubbed down with precious oils and spices, he is constantly stroked and pampered by a multitude of beautiful women, he dines on lavish foods, he plays his saxophone, has sex, and drinks all day and night. He is in a constant state of overload and, one day when he is making love with three women at once while the Princess looks on, captivated, he pulls away, eyes wide and wild, crying out that he has had enough. This scene and the following conversation between Phelps and Princess Lai Me illustrate De Sandra's much-publicized belief that complaining about one's success makes one a slave to the very source of their complaint, hence force making it imperative to give gratitude for every victory, for every achievement. In this instance, Phelps was enslaved and forced to participate in those activities in which he had previously over-indulged. His excessive life had become a literal prison, and, ironically, to survive in this prison he had to indulge in the activities that were his downfall in the first place, those things which had previously nearly taken his life. Before his awakening, he had forgotten what he loved, what he lived for. It was all an empty ritual. He was trapped.

However, at the moment Phelps' eyes are opened to the truth and he desires to be free once more, both literally and figuratively, the urge to live, to truly live *Pura Vida*, his soul is moved to action. He confronts Princess Lai Me and demands to be set free. In one of the film's more stirring monologues, Phelps proclaims that he would rather be free and live a life of uncertainty than be in bondage and live a life of luxury. De Sandra has been criticized for this scene, as some claim it is too "preachy", but its emotional effectiveness and universally recognized message of hope and liberty quickly quiets such accusations. In the end, it is one man standing up for his beliefs and being proactive in his fate, thus displaying another deeply held ideal of the director, that we do have a say in the direction and outcome of our lives.

Seeing an opportunity, the Princess agrees to set Blondie free if he can give her something that she has never been able to have: an orgasm. Blondie agrees but adds that if he succeeds, the harem goes free as well. Although implied earlier, it becomes glaringly clear in this section of the film that the Princess represents sexual repression and fear of sexuality, as well as being a metaphor for religious sexual repression that hovers over modern society in which "we" are the "harem", the "harem" is "us", a people captive and held at bay, our own needs and desires forced "underground", out of the light of "decent" society. The Princess processes her fantasies and desires by watching her female attendants make love with Blondie, but she never allows herself to participate due to her fear of love, of losing herself in another person, and of the vulnerability such actions and emotions would require.

What follows is perhaps the most highly regarded sex scene of all time; a forty-minute epic of non-stop sexy antics in which the Princess has thirty-seven consecutive orgasms, the very last of which is so powerful that her full and exhausted heart explodes, and she dies. It is a sad irony that finally opening up and sharing her body and spirit is what kills her. She literally "gives" her heart to Blondie as she grants him his freedom.

In the film's closing act, as Blondie leads the harem out of the underground lair and into the bright morning sun, the pale women squinting and shielding their eyes from the light, a sense of bittersweet victory falls over the proceedings; yes, Blondie has won freedom for himself and the harem, but where will they go, what will they do? Looks of both wonder and dismay color the features of the lost woman whose future is now so open and free, yet so frightening and uncertain. It is at this moment that Chaz Luger delivers his most famous and well-loved line.

"Go now, gentle sluts! You are free from the tyranny of the Princess! Free to laugh, free to live... free to fuck!" He shouts as the women file out into the city streets. It is in these final moments of the film, wherein a joyful Blondie watches the former servants step into their autonomy, that De Sandra's message of individuality and empowerment once again rings loud and clear.

We have already seen arguments for self-acceptance with Blondie learning to live with and love his penis fingers, as well as the idea that a perceived "handicap" can prove to be an asset, that an "abnormality" may improve an individual rather than hinder them. This belief comes to life in Phelps' ascent to super-stardom after acquiring the penis fingers. In Blondie's excessive, palatial life and his underground incarceration, we see that in both instances he was a slave to his passions and vices, whether they were of his choosing or were forced upon him, thus illustrating the concept of empty pleasures being a trap, a snare that is set by an ungrateful attitude regarding personal achievements and universal blessings. It is also here that De Sandra argues for recognition of the inherent spirituality in physical love and the intrinsic value of such. Lastly, through the Princess, we see De Sandra's belief in the destructive harm of sexual repression and shallow, loveless existence. We also see the belief that it is worth giving one's life to attain even a glimpse into a life of true love and pure passion. In the film's optimistic-but-not-completely-happy-ending, the message of absolute personal liberation despite the hardships it inevitably brings is seen. As the credits roll over an image of "Blondie" Phelps Martini playing his golden saxophone on a mountain top we know that this is a film about personal triumph, and that, no matter what we may think is in our way, there is a clear path for each of us on the mountain of life, and there is room at the top for us all.

"Transcribing the Prophetess"
A Conversation with Mandy De Sandra

. . . .

By

Harry Cox

. . . .

UPON MEETING MANDY De Sandra for the first time, one is immediately struck by her warmth, candor, and skillful use of innuendo. Perhaps these are the qualities that have contributed to her lengthy, storied, and highly successful career as a writer, filmmaker, and musician. Perhaps there is a mystical, undefinable quality at work? Maybe she's just lucky. Whatever the case may or may not be I was overwhelmed with delight when I was invited to meet with Ms. De Sandra and inquire of her for myself.

It was on a warm, late summer's day in 2016 that I was privileged to visit the iconic, multi-talented artist at the modest home she shares with her long-time partner, Trevor. Ms. De Sandra greeted me herself at the door of their home in suburban Washington, D.C., her mop of electric blue hair dancing atop her head and a smile shining across her bright face. She led me to the kitchen where Trevor stood at the island wearing his trademark sailor's cap, navy blue scarf, and black swim briefs, greeting me with a wink and a smile as he sliced limes for his secret recipe mixed drinks. Although it was only eight thirty-two A.M., I imagined this was the norm for artists and lovers such as these. After taking our seats in the cozy breakfast nook that sat nestled inside a looming bay window, Trevor served us our drinks and retired to the adjacent rumpus room to look at photos of his yacht. While sharing a smile with Ms. De Sandra, we both took the first sips of our drinks. As warmth filled my chest, I turned on my digital recorder and we began to discuss the work that is considered by many to be her finest hour as a filmmaker, the critically lauded, much-celebrated *Friday Night Fuckfest in F Minor.*

Harry Cox – What were the circumstances surrounding the making of *Friday Night...*?

Mandy De Sandra – Like Kenneth Anger, I decided to do a chaos magick spell to make sure men start evolving with dick fingers. Men are best with their hands, and I believed that playing a show and then crowd-surfing on a bunch of dick fingers would be euphoric.

HC – It was your sixty-ninth film. When approaching the project, did you see it as a milestone in your career?

MDS – I see all. I knew to make my Gnostic Gospel complete; films would have to capture the words on pages.

HC – At the time of the making of FNFFIFM, where did you feel you were in terms of your artistic evolution? Was FNFFIFM an important step in that evolution, in that growth process?

MDS – Could I make a film that would give people powerful erections (clitoral as well) along with even more powerful empathy? To bring my mission to a fold I must reach those who even refused to read. My growth as the most important artist of the century showed I had to show the world that life is a Friday Night Fuckfest in F-Minor.

HC – Was there any particular inspiration behind the story?

MDS – Sisyphus' erection.

HC – You are a highly regarded rock musician. How do you feel about smooth jazz?

MDS – It dries my vagina, but I like it when smoking bath salts.

HC – Your insistence that in every musical performance scene, the instruments be played by the actors and recorded live on set with no overdubs has been seen as a bold artistic statement. Why this choice? Did the actors have to learn their respective instruments or were they chosen for the roles because they were already trained as musicians?

MDS – That was the only way for the chaos magick spell to work. Through my direction, I can mold a man to play songs for the gods.

HC – Why did you choose to adhere to a strict "No CGI" policy? What was it like working with practical, "old school" on-set and in-camera special effects?

MDS – CGI is the Viagra of film-making. I want real boners and real scenes. Whether film or boners, we should never fake either.

HC – Whereas most adult films revel in fantasy and avoidance, practically everything about FNFFIFM has a gritty, documentary feel to it. Why this choice?

MDS – While my stories are fantastical, films must capture the truth of man. That is the only way to turn them all into the True Gnostic Gospel.

HC – Why the use of improvised dialog and non-choreographed sex scenes? Was this the influence of the music, the free-form of jazz, carrying over into the acting and the actual filming of the scenes?

MDS – Whatever is real, whatever is a want, the camera must catch. The actors are but mirrors into my truth.

HC – What was it like working with Chaz Luger in his debut role?

MDS – Similar to being in a gangbang by Denny's.

HC – How was your experience filming on location in Mable Town? Why did you choose this location?

MDS – For tax purposes.

HC – Many critics have argued that the film is an indictment of American society and its inherent hypocrisy as a culture of religious repression and simultaneous sexual obsession. Do you feel that this is a fair assessment?

MDS – I AM America.

HC – Were you consciously trying to make any sort of statement regarding sexuality with the film, be it personal, social, or otherwise?

MDS – Everything I do is sexual. Sexuality is the only truth in the universe.

HC – With six weeks in pre-production, forty-two days of principal photography, and seven weeks in post, you spent what is considered by adult filmmaking standards to be an unbelievably absurd amount of time making FNFFIFM. Why spend so much time on this particular film?

MDS – Why did the Demiurge only take 7 days to make the Earth that was billions of years in human time? Because Gods and goddesses get shit done.

HC – How did you become involved with New Kink Pictures?

MDS – I gave Nick and Don hand jobs at Denny's.

HC – At the time, did you know that FNFFIFM would be your last film?

MDS – Like Christ, I've always known when my time is up.

HC – The film's tenth anniversary is fast approaching. How do feel about the influence it's had and the impact it has made?

MDS – I am beyond ego and three-dimensional views of influence and impact. The film was and is and always will be.

HC – Do you see the film continuing to reach and affect future generations?

MDS – I know the University of Mars will study it.

HC – Are there any plans for a special 10th anniversary DVD or Blu-Ray release? Perhaps a theatrical re-release? There are rumors concerning the so-called "lost" two-hundred and thirty-six hours of footage being released as extras as well as a possible director's cut. Can we expect anything new for this anniversary?

MDS – Some truths I cannot share, but if that were to happen... It would be a film in the vein of Infinite Jest.

HC – As our time appears to have drawn to a close and I am so buzzed from this drink that Trevor made that I can hardly see, do you have any parting words of advice for aspiring adult filmmakers?

MDS – Do the work and get better. Life is but a dick and we must enjoy the highs and the lows.

HC – Ms. De Sandra, thank you very, very much for your kindness, hospitality, and generosity with your time. It truly has been an honor to speak with you today.

MDS – You sir are a gentleman and a scholar. Thank you and may you know Gnostic Bliss.

• • • •

SHORTLY AFTER OUR CLOSING words and pleasantries were exchanged, my world faded into a haze and I awoke, naked from the waist down, on a spaceship where a giant pink Maine Coon cat was licking my forehead. Later that day I was dropped off on the Jersey shore where I quickly made friends with some wonderfully kind and colorful locals who assisted me by buying me a pair of pants and a bus ticket back to Mable Town. Truly, it was an adventure that this humble scribe shan't soon forget.

*This article first appeared on September 4th, 2016, in the Sunday edition of the West Side's most esteemed tabloid, *The Mable Town Know-it-All*. It is reprinted here with the kind permission of its original publishers.

Author's Note (Hey, that's me, y'all!)

This is a new version of an old book. The original title is *Crust,* and it was published by New Kink Books, an imprint of Rooster Republic Press, on March 24, 2017. Then, in 2019, New Kink was discontinued and *Crust* went out of print. But even though it didn't last very long, working with New Kink and getting published by them was a very positive experience. Everyone there was super cool and totally nice to me, even when I accidentally sent them the wrong version of *Crust* without the supplemental material, which left a lot of details in the main story unexplained. I didn't notice until I received the author copies that I'd ordered. Oops! So, the book had to be pulled, reformatted, and republished. And they didn't fire me or cuss at me or even put a hex on me! I am forever grateful for the patience and kindness of Jeff O'Brien, Nick Day, and Don Noble, for giving me a shot and for being so effing cool to me. I learned a lot and it was wonderful getting to work with them for that brief period. I even earned $10! This is very significant because it's the first royalty check I ever received for my writing. I still have it in the top drawer of my desk.

Anyhow, about the book... In 2015 I was working second shift at a computer parts recycling warehouse in Lithia Springs, Georgia. I'd just quit smoking, so, instead of rushing outside to burn my lungs away during the second half of my half-hour lunch break, I stayed inside and wrote. And this book is what I wrote. Although I started with some sort of bizarro erotica in mind, I feel like this book ended up being more of a satire. Whatever it is, I had fun writing it and I hope you had fun reading it. Writing this stuff was a huge help in keeping my mind off of cigarettes. Christoph Paul once said that writing is good medicine. I totally agree and I'm grateful to be able to do it. Thank you so, so much for reading this silly little book and this little author's rambling, too. I hope that all is well in your world, and I thank you for being a part of mine.

I gotta go. If you read all this, you rule forever. I can't thank you enough, I wish I could.

Your friend,

Russell

Sunday, February 4, 2024

4:10 p.m.

Did you love *Piper and Shelly and the Weird Thing That Happened*? Then you should read *Wanda the Bloodtose Intolerant Vampire*[1] by Russell Holbrook!

[2]

DANCE, DANCE, DANCE!!!!!

In the heart of Mable Town, there is a sweet and irreverent love story blooming!

All teenage Wanda wants is to be a part of the local vampire dance troupe, Blood Waltz - the acclaimed free-form avant garde group that actually doesn't do any waltzing at all. With their dark and mysterious allure, they captivate Wanda's imagination and he yearns to join their ranks. However, Wanda's overbearing mother is vehemently against vampires, especially dancing ones, and forbids her son from having anything to do with them. But mothers don't always know what's best,

1. https://books2read.com/u/mv6GWJ

2. https://books2read.com/u/mv6GWJ

do they? Despite her mother's disapproval, Wanda rebels and sneaks out to attend a Blood Waltz performance. Little does he know that this act of defiance will have disastrous consequences, leading him down a dark path seeking vengeance against a rival dancer. As Wanda grapples with he newfound bloodlust and struggles to maintain control, he must also navigate the complicated waters of teenage love. Will Wanda be able to redeem himself and see his dreams of joining Blood Waltz come true? Can love, and dance, conquer all, or will vampiric desires prevail in the end? In this heartwarming tale of forbidden love and redemption, we are reminded not to give up on our dreams - or our shoes - no matter how dark life (or the dance floor) may get!

Also by Russell Holbrook

Heroin is the Answer: A Memoir of What I Can Remember
Lucy Furr
The Distended Table: A Collection of Holiday Favorites
Wanda the Bloodtose Intolerant Vampire
Piper and Shelly and the Weird Thing That Happened

About the Author

Staff writer #001428, Russell Holbrook, writes books, stories, and music exclusively for the glory of Valkos Enterprises Department of Letters and Distractionary Materials. He has been a faithful and steadfast employee of the division since 1989 when, as a teenager, he was moved from his assignment on the conveyor line at the Valkos computer parts recycling supercenter to the Writers of Distractionary Materials warehouse where he continues to occupy his very own desk with an inspirational cactus, under a small window on the 17th floor. He lives in West Mable Town with his legally registered life partner and their five furry children.

About the Publisher

Established in 2017 by Svaden Von Valkos III, Splatterpiece Press is a boutique publisher specializing in the bizarre and macabre. It operates under the Valkos Enterprises Department of Letters and Distractionary Materials, a branch of the Valkos Enterprises Division of Entertainment and Programming Propaganda. Having left his job as a lead dishwasher at Fun n' Games Family Fun Center, Svaden reluctantly joined the family business after being promised the opportunity to run his own division. With a small team and grand ambitions, he began releasing their dark creations into the world.